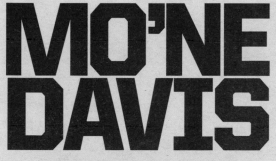

MO'NE DAVIS

REMEMBER MY NAME

MY STORY FROM FIRST PITCH TO GAME CHANGER

with Hilary Beard

HARPER

An Imprint of HarperCollinsPublishers

Mo'ne Davis: Remember My Name

Library of Congress Control Number: 2014958853
ISBN 978-0-06-239754-6

16 17 18 19 20   CG/OPM   10 9 8 7 6 5 4 3 2
❖
First paperback edition, 2016

To inner-city kids who need opportunities

CONTENTS

MO'NE DAVIS

REMEMBER MY NAME

MY STORY FROM FIRST PITCH TO GAME CHANGER

INTRODUCTION

MY NAME IS MO'NE DAVIS. SOME PEOPLE KNOW ME AS THE first girl to throw a shutout in the Little League Baseball World Series. I am only the fourth American girl and the eighteenth girl from anywhere in the entire world to ever get to participate. Other people know that I was the first Little Leaguer and the youngest athlete to be on the cover of *Sports Illustrated* magazine. I was named SportsKid of the Year by *Sports Illustrated Kids*, too. And still others know me as the girl who read *'Twas the Night Before Christmas* with the First Lady of the United States.

My teammates, who I've played with since I was seven, know more about me than almost anyone in the world. They know that I always try to make people feel good and cheer them up when they're mad or upset. They know that I tell a lot of cheesy jokes. And even though I'm a good athlete, sometimes I'm goofy and clumsy. My catcher, Scott, still cracks up about the time that I walked into a pole.

Opposing batters? Well, they know that I throw a nasty curve, a seventy-miles-per-hour fastball, and that I bring new meaning to the saying "You throw like a girl."

The summer of 2014, when I turned thirteen, I played in the Little League World Series and had the best time I've ever had in my young life. Me and some of my teammates from my Philadelphia neighborhood baseball team, the Anderson Monarchs, also played on the Taney Dragons, our community's Little League all-star team. The Dragons first won our district tournament, then the sectionals, then states, then the regional tournament, and then we achieved every Little League player's dream: we went to the Little League World Series!

One hot August night that summer, I, Mo'ne—a girl who loves Disney movies, is afraid of the dark, and keeps change in her baseball pants pocket for good luck—stood on the pitcher's mound in front of 34,950 people and five million people from around the world who were watching on TV.

Even with all those eyes on our team, I didn't freak out. I just tuned out the crowd (I couldn't even hear my mom, who yells super loud!), stared straight into Scott's eyes, and fired strike after strike into his glove. *Pop!*

I gave up two infield hits and threw eight strikeouts against South Nashville that night. The Taney Dragons had shut out the second team in a row.

The fact that I was so calm under pressure and struck out so many boys amazed a lot of adults. It made people see girls who play sports in a different light, and turned me into a role model overnight. All of a sudden people started to recognize me, want my autograph, and remember my name.

CHAPTER 1
LUCKY SEVEN

"YOU'VE REALLY GOT A NICE ARM THERE," THE MAN SAID TO ME.

I was kind of surprised that anyone had been watching me, and I didn't know the man, so I just said, "Thanks," and looked away.

It was late October 2008, and I was playing catch with a football with my cousin Mark and some friends on the outfield at Marian Anderson, the neighborhood recreation center. Mark had just finished playing a baseball game and we were hanging out on the grass.

"It's okay, Mo, Coach Steve is my coach," Mark said. Mark is two years older than me.

"I'm sorry, I didn't mean to scare you," the man said.

"That's your name, Mo?"

"My name is Mo'ne," I answered, catching the ball. I aimed at the top of the silver skyscraper pointing into the blue sky over the tops of the trees, and threw the football back to Mark.

Anderson was just a few blocks from my house, but the field, it was like my backyard. It is this green oasis the size of a city block. A fence, parked cars, and, across the street, three-story redbrick row homes run all around it.

"Oh, Mo-NAY," he said, pronouncing my name carefully. "Nice to meet you, I'm Coach Steve."

"Hi," I said. Coach Steve's dark blue sweats had the word *Monarchs* in white across the chest. A yellow pencil balanced behind his ear. For a split second I wondered if it ever fell off.

"How old are you?"

"Seven."

"You've got a really strong arm. Most boys your age can't throw as far as you can," he said. "I'm starting a Monarchs team for seven-year-olds. It's a boys' team, but you can play if you want. Why don't you think about coming out to basketball practice?"

"Okay," I said, looking him in the eye for the first time. He looked kind. Lots of kids played for the Monarchs. And I liked basketball. A lot.

Then he took the pencil and wrote on a scrap of paper

he pulled out of his pocket.

"Will you give this to your mother and ask her to call me?"

"Okay." I smiled at him, and carefully put the paper in my front pocket.

Later on, after I rode my bike home, I uncrumpled the paper and handed it to my mom.

"What's this?" she asked me. She was roasting a chicken, baking macaroni and cheese, and mashing sweet potatoes—my all-time favorite dinner—and the house smelled really good. My little brother, Maurice, who is four years younger than me, was watching cartoons on the couch.

"This man wants you to call him," I told her.

"Who is he? You shouldn't just be talking to strangers."

"He isn't a stranger, he's Mark's baseball coach," I said. "He wants to invite me to play on a basketball team."

"Oh, okay, I'll call him," she said as she sprinkled some cinnamon into the sweet potato pot. Yum!

I hoped my mom would pick up the phone while she cooked. But she didn't. She didn't pick it up then, or when she washed the dishes, or when we were watching TV later on that night.

"Mom, you gotta call that man," I reminded her the next morning when I put on my uniform for school.

"Okay, I will."

When I got home after school, I asked her again.

"Did you call that man yet?"

"Not yet."

"When are you going to call him?"

"Soon."

It turns out that my mom wasn't exactly thrilled about me playing what she saw as an aggressive sport. When I was a baby, she thought that I would become a girlie girl—the kind who would like dressing up, and getting her hair braided and curled, and playing with dolls. But I wasn't that girl. My mom says whenever she would buy me a doll, I would just look at her like she was crazy. I'd rather run around with a football or basketball and try to keep up with my brother Qu'ran, who is four years older than me.

"I was a big Allen Iverson fan," says Qu'ran. "So I started playing basketball, and she saw me dribbling and found it attractive, and started doing the same thing."

People say I look just like Qu'ran. You could say he is the boy version of me.

The next day, I tried with my mother again.

"Mom, you gotta call that man."

"All right, Mo'ne, I'm gonna call."

When I came home from school, she picked up the phone and started dialing Coach Steve.

"My daughter, Mo'ne, gave me a piece of paper with

your name and number on it and said that you wanted me to call you," she said as she sat in a kitchen chair.

I leaned up against her so I could listen.

"Oh, yeah, hi, my name is Steve Bandura. I coach the Anderson Monarchs. I was watching your daughter play football the other day."

"Football! Mo'ne's playing football?" My mother frowned. My mom, she's the kind of person who sometimes fusses a lot, but even when she's yelling, you can do something funny and make her laugh.

"She was just throwing the ball around with her cousin Mark, who I coach on the Monarchs, and some of their friends," Coach Steve said.

"Oh, okay." My mother relaxed.

"I've never seen anyone throw like that at her age— boy or girl—and I've been coaching kids for a long time."

"I didn't even know Mo'ne could throw a football," she said, raising one eyebrow and giving me a side-eye.

A few weeks before, I had talked to her about football. Qu'ran had taught me how to throw a football.

My friend Qayyah and I wanted to play for the South Philly Hurricanes at Smith Playground.

"Her mom said that if my mom let me play, she could play. And my mom said, if her mom let her play, I could play," Qayyah says. "But then they wouldn't let us."

"Not many kids that age can throw a football, because the ball's so big and their hands are so small. But Mo'ne was throwing the ball about twenty yards," Coach Steve told my mom. "I'm starting a Monarchs team of seven-year-olds. It's all boys, but I invited her to come to basketball practice."

"You want Mo'ne to play on a basketball team with all boys?!" My mother started to talk very fast, like she does when she gets worked up.

"Your daughter's got something special," he said.

"But playing with boys—I don't want my daughter getting hurt!"

"They're just seven. There's not a lot of physical contact."

"Oh, okay." I could feel my mom calming down. "Thank you very much. I'll think about it and get back to you," she said, and hung up the phone.

"Mo'ne, you wanna go?"

I broke into a smile.

"Yes!"

Even though she didn't like the idea of me playing with boys, my mom took me to practice the very next day. I didn't know it then, but when I look back on it now, the year I turned seven was the year that I started having good luck.

CHAPTER 2

ALL EYES ON ME

WHEN MY MOM AND I WALKED INTO THE GYM, THE FIRST thing I thought was that it was hot. The second thing I noticed was the smell of dirty socks.

Coach Steve and the team were already on the basketball court when my mom and I got there. As we cut across the corner of the court and headed toward the bench, it seemed like the grown-ups in the stands and along the court were staring at us.

Coach Steve said something to the team, then walked off the court and came over to greet us.

"Hi, I'm Lakeisha," my mom said as she reached out her hand. "I guess you already know Mo'ne."

"Nice to meet you, Lakeisha. Thanks so much for letting Mo'ne come," he said, before smiling at me. "Great to see you, Mo'ne. You ready to have some fun?"

"Yes." I smiled back at him, feeling excited but shy.

"I see they're all boys . . . ," my mother said. I could tell by the sound of her voice that she was nervous.

"Yes, we have twelve boys on the team. Most of them have been with us since they were four, so I know them very well," Coach said. "That one over there, in the navy blue Monarchs T-shirt, is my son, Scott. They're all very nice kids, and a lot of them have been together since they were three or four—they're like family to each other. You don't have to worry; they won't be mean to Mo'ne or give her any trouble."

"Okay, that's good to know," my mom said, relaxing.

"If it's okay with you, I'd like to get her started with practice," Coach said.

"That's fine," she said. "I'll stay for a little while to make sure she's okay. But I have to go to work. My boyfriend, Mark—we call him Squirt—is gonna pick her up."

"Okay, no problem," Coach said.

My mom smiled, gave me a hug, and then walked toward the sidelines.

Coach Steve put his hand on my shoulder and turned me toward the court. He told me the boys were doing something called a three-man weave.

"You don't have to do this drill; it's a little tough. You can wait till the next one," Coach Steve said, watching me. "But watch for a while, and let me know if you want to try."

The boys stood in three lines facing one of the baskets. The boy in the center passed the ball to the boy on his right, then ran on a diagonal line to the right and toward the basket. The boy on the right side passed the ball all the way across the court, to the boy on the left, then ran across to the left and toward the basket. The kid who had been on the left headed toward the middle. He caught the ball, bounced it, and took a shot. The ball bounced off the side of the hoop.

"Nice job, boys!" Coach Steve yelled.

Coach kept looking over at me while I watched the boys repeat the drill a couple of times and listened to the sound of their sneakers squeaking on the hardwood floor. The three-man weave looked like fun, and it didn't seem that hard to me.

"What do you think?" Coach asked.

"I could try it," I said.

"Already!" He seemed surprised. "Are you positive?"

I nodded.

Coach walked me onto the court, put his hands on both my shoulders, and guided me into a line.

"Guys, this is Mo'ne," he said. "She's going to be joining us."

"Hey," a few of them said.

The kid Coach Steve had pointed out as his son said, "I'm Scott. Nice to meet you."

"Hey," I said. I'm kind of shy at first.

When it was my turn to go, a kid threw me the ball. I threw it across to the kid on the other side, and ran across the court. That kid threw it back across the court and the first kid shot. This time, the ball went in.

"Nice job, Mo'ne!" Coach Steve yelled, clapping his hands.

This boy reached out his hand to give me a low five.

"Nice pass," he said.

"Thanks."

I looked over at my mom, who yelled, "Go Mo'ne!"

I saw some of the men near her pointing in my direction.

"You okay?" she asked.

I nodded.

"Okay, I've gotta go to work," she said. "Squirt will pick you up when practice is over." Squirt is now my stepdad, but they weren't yet married back then. His real name is Mark—I have no idea why everyone calls him Squirt. Then my mom waved and left.

Coach Steve couldn't believe how quickly I caught on. Neither could the boys.

"Wow, you learned that fast," Scott said, impressed. Later on, Scott told me that his dad had already told him about me.

"My dad had told me that this girl would be coming to practice and to make her feel welcome and treat her like family," Scott says. "He told me she would be awesome."

Coach set up the next drill. I watched, then joined in.

It was awesome, just like a fun game.

After practice ended, I was kind of tired, but really excited. The other kids told me their names. This boy named Jahli told me I did a great job.

"What did you say your name was again?" one of the boys asked.

"My name is Mo'ne."

"Wait, Monie?"

"No, Mo'ne."

"Sorry, next time I'll remember."

When practice ended, Squirt gave me a big hug.

"I saw the end of practice," he told me. "You did great!"

"It was really fun," I told him. "Can I come back?"

Before Squirt could answer, Coach Steve came over. "Are you Squirt?" he asked.

"Yes, I'm picking up Mo'ne," Squirt answered.

"Okay, I just wanted to make certain," Coach said. "I'm Steve Bandura, and I'm the Monarchs' coach."

"Great to meet you, Coach!"

"I just wanna tell you, nobody learns those drills that fast. Mo'ne has really got a gift!"

"Yeah, she's something else!" Squirt said. "Thanks for saying that."

"I hope you bring her back," Coach said.

"You wanna come back, Mo?" Squirt asked.

"Yes!"

I was really excited that practice had gone well. I could see myself coming here and playing with these kids again.

Squirt and I headed downstairs to the lobby. While we were walking, some of the adults said, "You've got quite a little player there," and "Nice practice," and things like that to us.

"She's all right, isn't she!" Squirt laughed.

One or two of them said, "You really gonna let her play with the boys?"

"Well, it looked like she could handle herself," Squirt told them.

I stood listening to the adults mix it up for a minute. Then I got bored and started looking around. I noticed this colorful painting across one of the walls. I had been in the rec center a lot, but for some reason I'd never seen this painting before. I walked across the lobby to look at it. It was a painting of a black lady and it stretched down the wall.

On the left side of the mural, the woman was standing in a long pink dress that looked almost like a wedding gown. I touched her dress, then dragged my fingers along the wall. In another part of the picture she was sitting at a desk, looking like she was daydreaming. The desk said *E. M. Stanton*. That was the name of the school one of my cousins went to, a block or two away. I wondered if she went there or if she was a teacher. In the middle of the picture there was a big white flower and the words *Marian Anderson at the Lincoln Memorial, Sunday, August 9, 1939*. Marian Anderson—I realized this was who our rec center was named after. On the right side of the flower, it looked like she was in a big, fancy theater, singing to people. Next to that, she was wearing a purple dress and a blue hat, sitting in the pews at church and singing. On the right end of the painting she was wrapped up in a blue-and-gold coat on top of her pink dress and smiling. In the background, people of all different colors were looking at her.

I heard Squirt's voice behind me. "You ready, Mo?"

"Okay."

As we were walking out of the recreation center, I realized that the big painting on the outside wall by the front door was the face of the same lady, singing. This picture was different—it was just the woman's head. There was a white circle around her, and flowers, birds, and blue skies behind her. She looked serious and like she knew what she was doing. I felt like the lady was looking at me like she was expecting something. A few years later I would learn we had a lot in common.

CHAPTER 3
NO EXCUSES, JUST RESULTS

THE OPPOSING PLAYER RAN INTO ME HARD, AND I FELL ON THE court and landed right on my knee. I grabbed it and started crying.

"You okay, Mo'ne?" Jahli asked as my teammates all huddled around me.

Coach Steve ran onto the court. "You all right, Mo?"

I could hardly answer him because I was crying.

Next thing I knew, my mom was standing beside us. "Are you okay, baby? Did you skin it?"

She must have run onto the court from the stands. But not everyone cared about how I was doing as much as my mom and my team did.

"Get off the court, *Mom*," I heard one of the fathers of the kids on the other team holler.

"You can't just run onto the court every time she gets hurt," another man shouted in a loud voice.

Now, my mom, she's not the kind of person you yell at. She can be feisty.

"Oh yes I can," my mom yelled back. "These boys are not gonna hurt my daughter."

Truth be told, my knee hurt a lot. But this had happened before—I played basketball with Qu'ran and his friends.

"I would tell her, 'You can't play with us. It's too hard and rough in this game,'" says Qu'ran. "She used to get mad and cry and stuff. So, finally, one day we let her play with us. She was out there playing rough, falling, scraping her knees. She'd get up, wipe it off, and keep playing."

"It isn't bleeding; you just have a bruise," my mom said.

I wiped my tears and stood up, and checked to see if I could walk okay.

"What do you think?" Coach asked. "You wanna sit on the bench and rest for a minute?"

"I'm okay," I said.

"I think you should go sit down," my mom said.

"No, I'm okay." I sniffled.

"You don't have to play," Coach said.

I didn't think twice about it.

"I want to stay in," I told them, and Mom went back to the stands and Coach Steve went to the bench.

Scott and all of my teammates gave me five. "You're gonna be okay," Scott said.

I was officially an Anderson Monarch. I had felt like a regular member of the Monarchs from the start of my very first practice, and now I was an important part of their games. When the team practiced, I practiced. When the team played, I played. When the team won or lost, so did I. Coach had taught my teammates to make new people feel welcome, and that included me.

There are a lot of different activities at Anderson: baseball, basketball, football, soccer, boxing, swimming, dance. Some of the kids who were really good athletes got to play on the Monarchs. The Monarchs are a travel team that plays baseball, basketball, and indoor and outdoor soccer.

Coach Steve has been running the Monarchs since way back when my mom was in high school. He wanted to give inner-city children whose parents didn't have a lot of money the chance to compete on travel teams just like children with more money do. Coach, he really has a passion for baseball. For some reason, a lot of people think that African American kids don't want to play baseball. This doesn't make any sense to Coach, and he likes to prove them wrong.

A lot of my teammates on the Monarchs had known each other since they were three or four because their older siblings played on Coach's T-ball teams. By the time I met him, Coach Steve knew or had coached almost everyone in the neighborhood, including my cousin Mark. Everybody knew Coach Steve and everybody trusted him.

To play on the Monarchs you had to play all three sports, even if you weren't that good at all of them.

"If we had tryouts for each sport, we might win more games," Coach says. "But I think we're a better team because we're like a family."

The Monarchs also have to practice good sportsmanship and take pride in being on the team. I liked doing those things. The Monarchs were my team now, for as long as I wanted to be part of it.

I practiced basketball with the Monarchs three days a week, plus had games on top of that. Lots of times my mom brought me, but Squirt grew up playing football and basketball, and he would bring me, too. My mom had mixed feelings about me playing sports. On one hand, she didn't have a problem with me playing, or even playing with the boys. On the other hand, she didn't like the fact that I played sports with so much physical contact.

When she was in junior high school, she had run track, which doesn't have any physical contact at all.

My mom also had a problem with sports because of my hair. In case you don't know this, hair care is a major dilemma that keeps a lot of African American girls from playing sports. Most black girls' hair is naturally very thick and curly. When we sweat or our hair gets wet, it gets even curlier and can be very hard to manage.

"I didn't want her hair to look messed up, and I didn't want to use chemicals to straighten it," says my mom. So she braided my hair and put colored beads and barrettes in it, and sometimes Miss Martina, her hairdresser, would braid it and curl the ends. Calling adult friends of the family "Miss" or "Mr.," or "Uncle" or "Aunt"—that's how a lot of African American children show their love and respect.

A few weeks after basketball started, we started learning baseball, so my mom bought me a brand-new pink-and-purple glove. I had never worn a baseball glove before, so Coach Steve had to explain how to put it on. I had played with a tennis ball, but I had never thrown or caught a baseball. Or maybe I had, but I hadn't really been paying attention.

One day, Coach opened a door in the wall with the picture of Marian Anderson painted on it and we went into this big room on the first floor that I had never been in before. Coach called it the indoor pitching and batting cage. The room was really big, and all these nets were hanging down from the ceiling. There were mirrors on the walls, with lines of red and black tape on them. And on the wall were little posters about ideas that Coach would always talk to us about: *Attitude is everything. Work hard, good things will happen. No excuses, just results.*

Coach Steve told us to get in line, then he handed me the ball, backed up, and told me how to throw. No sweat. Then he threw the ball back at me. To hear him tell it, me catching the ball for the first time was a big deal.

He says, "Just as the ball was leaving my hand, I thought, 'Oh no, she's never worn a glove before!'"

Most kids who have never worn a glove try to catch the ball with their wrist facing up and the web of the glove facing down. If the ball is coming straight at them, it will hit the glove and bounce right up into their face.

"I was cringing because I threw it next to her head," he says.

But I reached for the ball with the web of my mitt up and caught it. Then I turned and got in the back of the line.

"It was like she had been wearing a glove her entire life. It was unbelievable," Coach says.

In the indoor cages, we moved from station to station. The boys had all played T-ball before, so they already knew how to hit and throw.

There was this machine that threw balls at you. It would throw twenty to your right-hand side, twenty to your left, twenty up high, and twenty below. We would practice fielding the ball.

Then we would practice batting off of a hitting tee. Coach Steve showed me how to set my feet, lower my left shoulder, and drive my hips through as I swung. It took me a minute to get it, but I started being able to hit the ball. The nets hanging from the ceiling kept everyone from hitting each other with the ball and getting hit.

Coach taught every kid how to play every position in every sport. So I learned how to catch. I also learned to pitch and play first base, shortstop, and third base. In basketball, I usually play point guard, but I can also play center. Later that year, when we learned how to play soccer, I learned to play forward, midfielder, defender, and goalie. In the beginning, soccer wasn't my favorite sport, but when I got older, I started liking it a lot more.

When I was pitching, sometimes Coach would film me. Then he would show me how major league players threw, and have me compare my motion to a major league player's motion.

"Lift your elbow up, Mo'ne," he would tell me.

I'd lift it. *Strike!*

Coach says that he started noticing little things about

me. Things like how quickly I would pick up something new, like fielding ground balls from every position; that I had a natural whip in my shoulder when I pitched; how things that were usually hard to learn seemed effortless to me.

I don't remember a lot about when I first started competing in games, but Scott and Jahli say they remember.

"When you looked around, you would see everybody's eyes pop open really big," Jahli says. "I even saw some fans' jaws drop looking at her."

"And they would stare," says Scott. "They would kind of whisper to each other and point, and ask each other, 'Do you think that's a girl?'"

"Then once we got on the court or on the field and she played how she does, it was even more shocking to everyone, how she became basically one of us," says Jahli.

Other than seeing people look surprised, I didn't really notice their reactions. Qayyah and her identical twin sister—her name is Yirah—had always played with the boys with me.

"There were a lot of boys in our neighborhood, so we had no choice," says Qayyah. "We were the only three girls."

Also, I don't know if it was always on purpose—sometimes I think they were just little kids and weren't that good—but my mom and Squirt say that some of the

boys on opposing teams played rough against me on purpose because I was a girl.

"It was one of those things like, you can't believe this
girl is better than you," Squirt tells me. "I'm gonna throw
an elbow; I'm gonna knock her down; I'm gonna try to
scare her away from this sport."

Basketball and soccer were the hardest sports for my
mom to watch.

"Every time I turned around, Mo'ne was on the
ground," she says. "The boys didn't care that she was a
girl. They used to beat up my baby—throw elbows, knock
her down—all the time. But soccer was the worst—they
used to kick her in the shins."

"I think they roughed her up to get back at her for
being a step ahead of them," Squirt says. "They tried to
scare her away, but she would jump right back in the
game."

I guess not every boy on the other teams we played
thought that girls should play sports with them, and
some of them felt embarrassed if I scored on them or if
they got outplayed. The boys in my neighborhood have
always treated me nicely, but they don't always like being
beaten by a girl, either.

"In basketball, if we make a move and they fall or
stumble, sometimes they will get mad or embarrassed
and just stop playing," says Yirah.

But I'm not out to embarrass anyone.

Coach Steve told us he didn't want us to play dirty. It was more important to him that we show good character and sportsmanship than it was that we win. Thankfully, my teammates were very protective of me, and most of the kids and teams were fair.

But not all of them.

With certain teams, elbowing was the least of our problems. Just so they could win, some of the kids would purposely kick our shins and knock us down on the ground when the ref wasn't looking—even when we were far away from the ball, way on the other side of the field.

Eventually, Coach taught us that we should expect dirty tricks from a handful of teams and kids. When those things happened, he would tell us to be physical right back. But when we started being more physical, we could tell that the other teams would get scared and become less aggressive. After we beat a couple of teams, the kids would refuse to shake our hands.

That's one of the most important things about sports. Everyone hates to lose, and everyone wants to win, but sometimes you're gonna lose—it happens to everybody, and it's just part of the game. So Coach teaches us to always have fun and not let our moods get too far up or down.

CHAPTER 4
THE RIGHT FIT

DURING THE WINTER OF 2008, JUST A FEW MONTHS AFTER I'D started playing for the Monarchs, Coach Steve had a conversation with my mom about school.

"Have you ever thought about putting Mo in a private school?" he asked her. Mo—that's what he calls me. People who know me call me Mo.

"No, I've never thought about it," she said.

Coach Steve had gotten my mother's attention. He didn't know it, but she had dropped out of high school when she was sixteen, when she got pregnant with Qu'ran. After Qu'ran was born, she worked at Taco Bell during the day and went to "twilight school" at night, to finish her high school education and get her diploma.

Because of her own experience, she thought it was especially important for her children to get a good education.

"I've been watching her and I think she really has a gift," Coach told her. "She's really good athletically, but she also has this ability to analyze what's happening on the basketball court, in a way that I've never seen before."

"Thank you," my mom told him. "I've always thought Mo'ne was really smart. She was on the honor roll in first grade and has been on it so far all through second grade."

"There's this great school that I think might be interested in her," Coach said, and he told my mom about the school that his daughter, Stephanie, went to. I had met Stephanie at the courts. "It's called Springside, and it is one of the top schools in the city. It's a girls' school—no boys would be in her classes."

Coach went on to tell her that the school's goal is to provide girls with a super education, but also to make them into strong people—girls with great ideas, great character, and great relationships with each other. A lot of other girls of color went there, and he thought it would be a great school for me and would prepare me to go on to college.

It turns out that Coach Steve was trying to make sure that all of the Monarchs went to good schools. In case you don't already know this, in a lot of cities—and especially in neighborhoods where people are poor—the schools aren't always as good as they are in many suburbs and parts of the city where people have more money. In the neighborhood I lived in, the teachers were nice, but the schools don't have enough money to give children the education they deserve. Some kids don't graduate from high school.

"Scott goes to Chestnut Hill Academy, the boys' school next door," Coach told my mom.

"I have never even heard of that school," my mother told him. Between working and raising me, my brothers, and my sister, my mom didn't start college until she was twenty-nine. She's been a certified nurses' aide since about the time that I was born, and now she's going to school to become a nurse. She's worked two jobs for her entire life. "I definitely want her to get a good education."

"We would have to get her tested to see if she can get in. IQ tests and other tests that prove that she can do the work—the school is very hard," he said.

"That sounds good to me," my mom said. "Just tell me what I have to do."

So Coach Steve and my mom took me to take these tests. I remember this friendly woman with blond hair, who looked like she had just graduated from college, had me play with some pop blocks.

Not too long after that, my mom told me that she and Coach were going to take me to visit this new school.

I liked the school from the minute we got there.

There were not a lot of trees in my neighborhood, but this school was located on the edge of a forest. It was April, and I remember that all the trees were super green. There were all these bushes around there with yellow flowers and bright pink flowers. And lots of grass—these really big sports fields were across the street. My school, Francis Scott Key Elementary School, was surrounded by concrete and brick row houses.

When we went inside, it surprised me that the floors were carpet. In my school, the floors were old and wooden, and if you stepped on certain parts the floor would creak. And this school was very spread out and on one level. My school had three different floors and you had to walk up and down the stairs.

I spent the whole day at Springside School going to second grade just like I would have in my regular school. Everyone I met treated me super nice. I remember that lots of adults and girls came up to me and introduced themselves and told me something about themselves. That's when I met my friends Abby, Allegra, Destiny, Nahla, and a lot of my other classmates. Then they asked me to tell them something about myself.

"My name is Mo'ne."

"Monique?"

"No, Mo'ne."

Then I told them where I went to school, and that I liked to play sports, and that I played on a team with the boys. Everyone seemed surprised almost every time I said that. I had a really fun day.

I thought I was going to go home that night and back to my regular school the next day. But after school was over, I found out that I was going to visit at Springside for one more day. My mom told me that she and Squirt had to go to work, so I would have to spend the night at Coach Steve's house, since Coach lives pretty close to the school.

Coach Steve and his wife, Miss Robin, were very nice, but I had really just met them and their family. I was a little nervous about the idea of staying overnight. But Scott and I played a board game, and that was fun. At bedtime, Miss Robin tucked me in with Stephanie, with Steph's head at one end of her twin bed and my head at the other. After Miss Robin turned out the light, I started crying.

"Are you scared of the dark?" Stephanie asked me.

"Yes, and I want my mom to come get me," I said.

"I'll get my mom," Stephanie told me, and she climbed out of bed and went to get Miss Robin.

"Steph came into our room and said, 'Mo'ne's crying,'"

Miss Robin says. My mom says I cried so much when I was a baby that it was hard to find anyone to help her take care of me. "I went into their room and she was whimpering. I told her, 'Oh, sweetie, I'm so sorry you feel so uncomfortable. Let me call your mom so you can talk to her.'"

Miss Robin called my mom. My mom was pretty matter-of-fact about the whole situation. She told me that she had to work, so she wasn't coming to get me. But it was important for me to visit the school for another day. I had to stick it out.

The next morning, Coach took me back to Springside and I spent another day there. I really liked it. About two weeks later my mother told me that I had been accepted and that they wanted me to start right away and finish second grade there, even though there were only six weeks left in the school year.

I was happy about going to Springside. And my mom was really glad I was going to get a great education. But I was also kind of nervous about starting my new school.

"I feel kind of bad about it, but when she first got here, people were like, 'Oh, snap! Somebody just came here in the middle of the school year. You can't come in the middle of the school year! That's not fair! Where did she come from? She can't do that!'" my friend Nahla remembers.

I didn't know it, but that had never happened before. All the other new kids had come at the beginning of the school year. But everyone was very nice to me, even though the year was almost over and everyone already had friends.

I didn't miss my old school at all, and I would still see my old friends around my neighborhood. But all of a sudden my mornings got kind of hard. For the last six weeks of second grade, I had to wake up super early and get in the car with my mom so that she could drive our silver Chevy Impala across the city to take me to school. Because it was rush hour, lots of times the ride would take almost an hour. After she dropped me off, my mom would drive all the way back to the house in rush hour traffic so she could pick up Qu'ran and take him to his school, and then take Maurice and Mahogany, who is six years younger than me, to day care. I know it wasn't easy.

I liked going to an all-girls school. One thing I liked was that the girls seemed to be very serious about their schoolwork, and I really liked to learn. I had been on the honor roll at Key, and I wanted to be on the honor roll at Springside. Also, we had this job chart in our classroom, and every week we had a responsibility—fun stuff like making sure the markers were sorted.

"When Mo'ne was added, the list became uneven and

someone had to take a week off," says Nahla. "Nobody wanted a week off."

But they were nice, and I didn't even know that there was a problem.

"From the moment she got there, she fit right in," my mom says.

One minute I'd talk to this person and the next minute I'd talk to that one. Allegra was one of the nicest to me out of all of them, and she became the very first friend I made. She always stood right behind me in line because both of our last names start with a *D*. Every day at lunch we would sit together, and I would eat my turkey and cheese sandwich. On Tuesdays and Thursdays, I'd bring a dollar so I could buy mint chocolate chip or chocolate ice cream from the cafeteria.

"They became friends because they were both very sporty," says Destiny.

"One recess, I was walking around the field with my friend Grace, and Mo'ne was throwing a football with Allegra," says Abby. "It was just them throwing the ball back and forth in the corner of the field, and that's the first thing I think about when I think of her. Mo'ne's always had a ball in her hand."

"Everything becomes sports," says Nahla. "She'll dribble a ball while she's eating."

"She'll toss a pencil case with you," says Destiny.

It's funny to hear my friends talk about me.

I did have to make some adjustments, though. Some of my new classmates told me they weren't used to my accent. I didn't think I had an accent. In fact, it kind of sounded to me like they had a little one. But I do remember thinking that I needed to improve my grammar. I kept listening to the proper way of speaking and practicing it over and over in my mind.

From the beginning, going to Springside caused my life to change in many ways. But those six weeks of second grade were a good introduction to the rest of my school experience there.

CHAPTER 5
CLASSY AND CLASSIC

THE KID TOOK A BIG RIP AT THE BALL AND HIT IT WAY OVER my head. I spun around on the pitcher's mound to watch how far it would fly. *Going* . . . The kid rounded first, and headed for second. The ball flew over our left fielder's head, then hit the ground and kept bouncing and rolling. *Going* . . . The kid rounded second and headed for third. At Parkwood Youth Organization in Northeast Philadelphia the field is open, and there isn't a fence. The batter swung around third, and crossed home plate before our guy had even picked up the ball. *Gone.*

It was 2008 and around the same time I started at Springside. This was my first time pitching in a real game.

We were only seven, but were playing up an age group. Coach Steve always played his teams one age group older, so we would get better. The kid who had hit the ball was only eight, but he was huge. So was his twin brother. Plus, back then, I wasn't throwing super hard. I didn't have a fastball and didn't know how to throw a curve. My main goal was just to get the ball over the plate.

After the ball was thrown back to me, I just stared down into my glove.

"I saw her head down and thought to myself, 'Uh-oh, she's crying,'" says Coach Steve. "I went out to the mound to talk to her."

I felt a hand on my shoulder and heard a soothing voice.

"You okay, Mo?" Coach Steve asked me.

"Yeah, I'm all right," I said, looking at him.

"When she looked up, she wasn't upset like crying; she was angry that this kid had hit a home run off of her," Coach Steve says.

He told me, "Everybody gets a home run hit off of them, so don't you let that get you down. Home runs are just part of what comes with being a pitcher."

"I'm okay," I said, spinning the ball in my hand in my mitt.

"Now just do what we've been practicing," he said. Then he rubbed my head through my baseball cap and walked back to the bench.

I didn't care if the kid was older and much bigger than me. Right there on the pitcher's mound, I made up my mind that the kid wasn't going to hit off me like that again. The next time he came up, I struck him out.

Coach was teaching us to be great competitors, but not to forget to have fun. What's the point of spending all this time together and playing a sport if it isn't fun? After the game was over, we all laughed about it.

"That ball flew halfway to New York!"

"You should have seen the look on Mo's face while she watched it!"

"The kid had scored, was in the dugout, and was drinking a Gatorade, and our outfielder was still out there in the weeds, looking for the ball!"

A few weeks after I'd joined the team, but before the baseball season began, Coach Steve handed me a book.

Jackie Robinson and the Story of All-Black Baseball.

"All of the kids on the Monarchs have read this," he told me. "I want you to read it, too."

On the cover, there was a picture of a black man, standing in front of a stadium, ready to swing a baseball bat.

"The book is about one of the greatest baseball players and greatest human beings who ever lived," Coach told me. "The Anderson Monarchs are named after Jackie Robinson's first baseball team, the Kansas City Monarchs. I want you to read this book, so you know what we stand for."

When I read about Jackie Robinson, I learned all sorts of new things. I learned that back around the time that my grandmother's mom was born, only white players were allowed in baseball's major leagues. But African American players wanted to play at that level, so they formed their own teams and played against each other in what they called Negro Leagues. (*Negro* is a word that people used to use to describe African Americans—it's really not a word you would use today.) The Negro League teams would travel by bus to big cities, smaller towns, and country areas to play other teams. They called these trips "barnstorming tours."

Back in the day of the Negro Leagues, baseball used to be *the* sport in the African American community, whether they lived in the city, suburbs, or country. Philadelphia had its own Negro League team, called the Philadelphia Stars.

After I read the book, Coach asked me to write a report about what I'd learned.

Some of the Negro League players were better than players in the major leagues. A lot of people said that Jackie Robinson was among the greatest of them all.

The general manager of the Brooklyn Dodgers wanted to have a winning team, so he signed Jackie Robinson to play for the Dodgers. On April 15, 1947, Jackie Robinson broke the color barrier and became the first African American player to compete in the major leagues. That year he became the National League's Rookie of the Year. Two years later, he was the National League MVP and won the batting title with a .342 average. Since then, a lot of African American players have played Major League Baseball. In fact, some of them—old-timers like Willie Mays and Hank Aaron, and new players like Matt Kemp—have become some of baseball's biggest stars. Coach wanted to start a baseball league so the Anderson Monarchs could carry on this important legacy.

He had us learn about Jackie Robinson to make the connection.

Jackie Robinson was African American and I was African American. Jackie Robinson's family was poor, and mine didn't have much money, either. And Jackie was a leader, and I was learning to lead. For a while, Jackie Robinson was the only black person in the MLB, and most of the time when I played, I was the only girl.

Jackie Robinson was also classy, even when people said and did mean things to him because he was black—and that happened a lot. So Coach taught us that we should be classy, too.

Our uniform was classic. We always wore white shirts with navy blue pinstripes and the word *Monarchs* written on it in navy blue. In baseball we wore throwback white with navy blue pinstripe pants and high socks, like the New York Yankees used to wear.

No matter what was going on, Coach Steve taught us how important it is to represent our team. We watch our behavior—we never want to do anything that would reflect badly on the Monarchs or our teammates. Like around Halloween, when some kids throw eggs at cars. Nobody on the Monarchs would like it if you did that. If you want to do something like that, you shouldn't be a Monarch.

One of the most important things Coach taught us was to not try to be fancy, but to learn the fundamentals of each sport. Like in baseball, we had to learn how to throw, how to catch, how to swing a bat, how to slide, how to pick a runner off a base, and how to turn a double play. Those are far more important than hitting a grand slam—a home run when there's a runner on every base.

In basketball, a lot of people really like it when a player slam-dunks. But that's not the most important part of the game. You have to do things like learn how to dribble with your right hand, dribble with your left hand, and throw a bounce pass. In soccer, it's the same thing— you need to know how to dribble and pass with both feet.

And since we couldn't afford fancy camps and specialized coaching like kids with more money could, Coach played us up an age group to give us better competition.

"We kept raising the bar, putting kids up against really good competition and playing a lot of games," he says.

We were never the biggest or strongest team.

And when he says we played a lot, he really means *a lot*. To give you an example, the Monarchs would play forty or fifty baseball games every year between April and the end of July, which is more than a lot of other teams play. Then we'd start fall baseball again in September and October and play another twenty games.

"We were running here, running there, carpooling, and the kids were spending the night at each other's houses," my mom says.

Another important thing Coach taught us was to develop a high sports IQ.

In baseball, "Coach Steve taught us to play small ball," Jahli says. "Bunting, stealing bases, making sacrifice flies, learning the pitcher and getting in his head. Playing Jackie Robinson's style of game."

Some kids like to "swing for the bleachers"—to try to hit a lot of home runs—but they tend to strike out a lot. That's not how we played. The point of our offense was to manufacture a run. We would do that at bat by at bat, pitch by pitch, hit by hit, play by play.

Here's an example of how it might go.

Usually Scott was our leadoff hitter—he would go first. Sometimes he would bunt—block back a pitch to create a little soft hit down the first- or third-base line. If he got on base, lots of times he would steal second base when the pitcher wasn't looking. Sometimes he would also steal third.

I would usually bat second, right behind Scott. If I could get a hit, Scott could usually score from whatever base he had stolen.

After I got on base, then I would try to steal second. If I made it all the way to third, I would take a lead off of third base, so I was closer to home plate.

Since I run pretty fast, Demetrius, who was on our team when we were younger and usually hit third, might hit a bunt also. Then I would try to sprint as fast as I could and make it to home plate. Sometimes, I'd even have to slide.

Safe!

Then the fourth batter would try to hit Demetrius in. This is how small ball goes—nobody came to bat trying to hit a home run. If we chipped away at things one play at a time, by the end of the first inning, we might be winning three or four to nothing. That's a good lead in baseball, since baseball is a hard game to score in. In soccer, scoring is also hard; in basketball, because the court is so small, it's easy to run up a lot of points.

But we didn't showboat—fist pump, chest bump, give a lot of high fives—or any of that. If there's one important thing to learn about sports, it's that losing is part of playing, so you always want to remember what it feels like to be on the losing team—not very good. I always try to put myself on the other side of the court and think about how the kids on the other team are feeling. That's one reason why, if we get a big lead, we don't rub it in. We've been in that situation before and it feels lousy.

In baseball, the main thing we wanted to do was to put the ball in play and keep it in play to put the pressure on our opponent's defense. Don't get yourself out by swinging at a pitch that you can't hit or by doing something that isn't smart, like getting picked off a base—thrown out because you're not paying attention. At our age we only play for six innings, so don't make any errors on defense while you're on the field. Offense wins games but defense wins championships.

Since we were spending so much time together playing sports, we were getting pretty good at working together, and at being a real team.

CHAPTER 6
FAMILY VALUES

BEFORE LONG, ALL OF THE MONARCHS AND THEIR PARENTS and siblings became like one big ole happy family to me. So, in 2011, everyone celebrated with my family when my mother and Squirt got married.

Mom and Squirt had been together for a while. When I started playing with the Monarchs, we already considered Squirt a part of our family. By then he and my mom had just had my little sister, Mahogany. A little while after Mahogany was born we had all moved into a house near Seventeenth and Manton. About a year after that, we moved into a three-bedroom house on Oakford near

Twenty-Fourth. Squirt, he also has a son and a daughter, who are the exact same ages as Qu'ran and me. His son spends a lot of time at our house. We have a big extended family.

About a year after Mahogany was born, Mom and Squirt, they got married. It was raining on their wedding day. That morning, my mom took all of her bridesmaids out to Perkins for breakfast, and Squirt took all the groomsmen to the barbershop to get their hair cut. Later that day we all went to the Merion, the catering place where the wedding was held. Mom had six bridesmaids, and I was her junior bridesmaid, so we had to start getting dressed pretty early.

I don't remember the wedding ceremony, except that I walked down the aisle with Squirt's son and my mom was late walking down the aisle. She walked down the aisle with Qu'ran.

Mom has a really beautiful picture of the wedding party posing on a staircase. In it, the bridesmaids are wearing lavender and lilac. Squirt and the groomsmen are wearing cream. I stand at the front of the brides-maids, wearing a long lavender dress and staring at my mom, who looks like a princess in her long white dress. Squirt stands on the other side of her, wearing a cream-colored tuxedo.

I remember a lot about the reception, I think because there was so much food. I had never seen anything like it before.

My mom and Squirt sat at a table at the front of the room, where all of us could see them. Maurice, Qu'ran, and I sat at the same table as Squirt's cousins. And Coach and Miss Robin and all of the parents of my Monarch teammates had come.

The food was really, really good. The waiters came around to ask what we wanted. First they brought us something to drink. Then they brought us a tiny scoop of sherbet ice cream. I had never seen anyone give you ice cream before dinner before!

Then they brought us some soup, and then another scoop of sherbet ice cream. The sherbet was really good. I liked it a lot.

Then they brought us our entrée—we could choose between chicken and beef.

Then more sherbet.

In the back of the room, there was this big ice sculpture of my mom's new last name and they had these fountains of liquid chocolate. They also had fruit, and all sorts of brownies and desserts. You could dip your fruit in the chocolate fountain.

And there was this big old dance floor. People started dancing. Of course, I taught 'em how to dougie. And toward the end of the night, the kids started playing hide-and-seek.

While my family was growing, my teammates were becoming like family, too.

The more time I spent with my teammates, the more I learned about their lives and cared about them. Take Scott, for example. I learned that on top of being really friendly and making you feel at home when you're new to the team, Scott is very intelligent and has a really high baseball IQ. He understands a lot about the game. In soccer, he's really smart with the ball. Basketball? Well, even he would tell you it's not his best sport. But he's one of the fastest on the team and takes pride in how much he's improved.

After a while Scott became like another brother to me. He knows that I don't like scary movies. He's seen me be goofy and we share funny Instagrams and Vines. He knows that I'm clumsy and that I like to walk around in my socks. He has seen me play basketball in the gym in my socks and slip and fall down on my butt.

"One time I was with her and she had way too much sugar," says Scott. "She kept running down the street and jumping around. We didn't know what she was doing. It was funny."

Sometimes I act kinda crazy at night.

"Then there was this time when we were playing

football and she hit this little girl in the head with the ball," says Scott.

I underthrew it.

"By, like, twenty feet," says Scott. "The little girl had been running past, and then she stopped and the ball hit her in the head."

I felt really bad about it. The little girl started crying and ran to tell her mom. Scott and a bunch of the other kids were laughing at me. Thank god her mom wasn't mad.

Scott and I have played together for so long that when we're on the baseball or soccer field or on the basketball court, we can just look at each other and know what the other one is thinking.

Then there's Jahli. He was really nice to me when I first joined the team. Like, when I didn't have a bat, he let me use his. If there's one thing you should know about baseball players, they're really picky about their bats. Jahli, he's a lot like Scott—very smart. So let's say you're batting and you're having problems hitting. He can look at your swing and tell you what's wrong with it—like you're swinging too late, or you're taking your eye off the ball. If you swing the bat too late, you'll only be able to hit a piece of the ball. Or you'll be limited to hitting to just one side of the field. If you swing really late, the ball will already be past you and you'll whiff—you'll swing and you'll miss. Jahli is also the kind of kid who, if something gets him upset, doesn't need anyone to tell him that he needs to calm himself down.

Carter, he's really nice and just super friendly—that's just how his personality is. And he's very funny. He has this thing he says, "Yeah, man," in a certain voice, and it makes us laugh. So every time we see each other we say that, "Yeah, man." And since Carter and I have the same last name, we're always joking with each other about who's the better Davis.

Even though we practice and play really hard, it's fun. That's why it's important that we have goofballs on our team. Sami is a really good player, but he's also the funniest person on our whole entire team. My mom has gotten really close to his mom, and now my family goes to the same church as his family. His grandfather is the pastor.

Myles has been on the team since he was three. Sometimes people call me Myles's mom. Especially in soccer, some of the opposing players mess with Myles because he's small, so he can get frustrated. When that happens, I always go over to help calm him down.

When I wasn't at school, I was almost always at Anderson or with the twins, Qayyah and Yirah. I would sleep on the bus on my way home from school, and when I got home I would do my homework. When I was done my mom would drop me off for baseball, basketball, or soccer practice. Sometimes I would finish my homework in one of the classrooms at Anderson.

Usually about once a week after practice, I'd see Miss Martina to get my hair braided and curled. The refs said the beads and barrettes I was wearing were causing them problems.

One time I was pitching and the opposing coach complained that my beads were distracting them because they were white. That was kind of ridiculous, but my teammate Nasir gave me one of his wristbands and I pulled back my hair. The other team didn't win.

Other times it was more embarrassing.

"They would make me take them out in the middle of the game," says my mom. "Then her braids would be sticking all over her head. I would be so mad. I would think, 'My daughter shouldn't have to look like this!'"

When I was nine or ten my mom gave in to the pressure from the refs and took me to get a chemical relaxer to straighten my hair.

"We tried a kiddie perm, but my baby's hair started breaking off and coming all out," my mom says. "From then on, I kept her hair natural and in braids."

Around that time Alicia Keys had the sides of her hair braided up toward the top of her head and a weave down the middle like a Mohawk. Miss Martina did my hair that way. We also tried other styles that I wouldn't sweat out and that didn't involve chemicals.

During the summer, I'd head over to Anderson, or sometimes the Christian Street YMCA or Chew Park, which are in South Philly, pretty much as soon as I rolled out of bed. Which can be in the middle of the afternoon.

"When Mo'ne stays with us, she gets up early," says Yirah. "When she's not with us, she wakes up at, like, two."

Qayyah and Yirah play basketball with the boys at the Y with me.

"We play three-on-three," says Yirah. "Me, Mo'ne, and my sister against the boys, like for ten games in a row."

"Sometimes boys think only they can play basketball," says Qayyah. "They say, 'Girls can't do that,' and then we show them that girls can do moves, too."

Qayyah, Yirah, and I dream of being in the WNBA. Every time we went to the gym together, we would say to each other, "One of us is going to be on TV and be famous."

A lot of good people live in my neighborhood, South Philadelphia. There are people of all different backgrounds: Italian, Irish, African American, Mexican, Chinese, Vietnamese, and Cambodian. The Sports Complex, where Philly's pro sports teams play, is there; so are two famous cheesesteak restaurants, Geno's Steak's and Pat's King of Steaks; a lot of Asian restaurants on Washington Avenue; and my favorite pizzeria, Lazaro's on South Street. Some famous celebrities come from South Philly, like Black Thought and Questlove from the hip-hop band the Roots; singers and songwriters like Patti LaBelle, Kenny Gamble, and Shawn Stockman and Nathan Morris from the group Boyz II Men; and Sylvester Stallone, who starred in the movie *Rocky*. My mom and Squirt were born here, too.

But not everyone can find a job, so a lot of people who live in South Philly struggle to have enough money. Sometimes there is a lot going on, and not all of it is good, so my mom is very protective. She never lets me walk to the Y or Anderson alone. I ride my bike with the twins, and lots of times Sami. Other times Squirt walks us over. Usually my mom, Squirt, or the twins' mom picks us up.

My mom says that the fact that I basically live at Anderson has helped protect me from some bad things that you hear about on the news but don't expect to happen near you.

"Mo'ne hasn't been around any fighting and shooting," my mother says.

I didn't even know that someone had been murdered in front of the store at the corner of my block.

This was my family and my town—my life. I woke up

every morning and went to school. I practiced hard with my teammates. I played pickup games with my friends. Everything was so great, I didn't imagine that soon even better days would come.

CHAPTER 7
FUNDAMENTALLY SPEAKING

IF YOU WANT TO GET BETTER AT SOMETHING OR FULFILL YOUR dreams, you have to work really hard, no matter whether it's in school, at sports, or another kind of dream.

Even though people know me for sports, getting my education is more important to me. I have been on the honor roll since I was in first grade, and I have worked hard to stay on it. Doing well in school makes you smarter and makes you feel good about yourself. It also helps you to get into college.

My school day starts every morning at 5:50 a.m. when my mom wakes me up. Well, actually, it starts the night before, when I take a bath and lay out my clothes—usually a sweatshirt or a collared shirt with the Springside logo on it, and either a blue plaid skirt, khaki pants, a blue skort, or the blue pants that I wear that make it not look so much like a uniform. Then I lay my socks on top of everything.

When it's time to wake up in the morning, I get right up.

"Well, it depends on who's waking her," says Qu'ran. "If I'm waking her up, she'll act different than if it's my mom waking her up. I wake her up on the weekends."

Mostly, I pretty much get up when Qu'ran wakes me, too.

"Last Saturday, when I woke her up she said, 'Why are you waking me up?' So I told her Mom said to, but then she waited, like, three minutes to get up," says Qu'ran.

Like I said, I get right up.

The school bus stops right in front of my house at 6:20, so I have to be ready when it gets here. By the time I get up, Squirt has already left for work. My mom, she works from four to midnight, so after she wakes me up, she goes back to sleep until she gets up with Qu'ran, Maurice, and Mahogany. Mahogany, she shares my bedroom. Thank god she sleeps hard, so when I get dressed she doesn't wake up.

If I didn't eat really late the night before, I go downstairs and make oatmeal or waffles. Waffles, they are my favorite breakfast—Eggo Homestyle Waffles with Aunt Jemima Butter Rich Syrup.

If there's one thing about my neighborhood, it's that it's really, really quiet, except on holidays like the Fourth of July, when people are cooking out and playing music. In the mornings I can hear the bus coming down the street. So I throw my bright pink knapsack with my books in it over one shoulder, my other pink knapsack with my baseball cleats and Monarchs uniform over the other shoulder, and carry my blue knapsack with my soccer cleats and practice clothes in my hands. My mom, she calls me the bag lady.

I climb onto the yellow school bus and say hi to our driver, Miss Denise. Then I throw my bags onto one seat, and flop onto another. I put on my headphones and try to go back to sleep.

"Mo'ne has to ride through the whole city," says Qu'ran. "It's an hour and a half to two hours each way, depending on traffic."

Miss Denise drives past the redbrick row houses on my street. There's a vacant lot a few doors down, where they tore down an abandoned house, and this really big empty brick warehouse at the end of the block. Then we turn right, drive under the bridge where the train goes over, and wind our way through Philadelphia. We drive along the edge of my neighborhood, which is called Point

Breeze, and near the museums along the edge of Center City—that's what Philly calls downtown. When we cross over the Benjamin Franklin Parkway, if you look to the left you can see the Philadelphia Museum of Art, where Sylvester Stallone ran up the steps in *Rocky*. To the right you see City Hall, which has a statue of William Penn on top of it. William Penn was the founder of Pennsylvania. There are a lot of things in Philly that are named after him.

A few blocks on the other side of City Hall you can see the landmarks where our nation was founded. Places like Independence Hall, where the Declaration of Independence was signed; the Betsy Ross House, where she sewed our nation's first flag; and stops along the Underground Railroad that helped black people escape from slavery.

Next, we drive over to Fairmount. After that we pick up my friend Senna, who's in my grade. If I'm still awake, me and Senna will talk. Senna, she talks loud and is very funny. Then the bus goes up to North Philadelphia, where we pick up Zion, who's on the Monarchs now. Then we cut over to Germantown.

"By the time I get on the bus, sometimes Mo'ne's asleep, sometimes she's up. I don't know how she does it," says Nahla. "Sometimes the bus is cold and she has her head against the window, her brother's Diego blanket to keep warm, and one leg straight and one leg bent and that foot up on the seat. Lots of times I'm bored, so I count how many times her foot falls off the seat. It's funny. Her foot falls off, and she just puts it back up on the seat, but she is dead asleep the whole time."

School starts at eight o'clock. We have advisory group, then first and second period, and then we have a snack in the cafeteria. Abby, Alexia, Destiny, and Nahla are in a lot of my classes, and we've been close for a long time.

"We laugh a lot, so it's good that we don't have all our classes together," says Nahla.

"Mo'ne laughs at everything," says Abby.

Everybody knows that school gets boring and people are tired in the morning and don't feel like going. That's one reason why I think you should be friends with a lot of people. Because even if you're bored, you've gotta think about the bigger picture, which is high school and college. Your friends will make the day go faster, you'll have a lot of fun, and you can work together to prepare for your projects, tests, and quizzes.

Lots of times Nahla, she's my work partner. I worry about my grades, but I'm not super worried. If I get, like, a B in a class that I should've gotten an A in, I know that I did something wrong. Most of the mistakes I make on tests, they're very like, "Oh, I knew this"—one of those small ones, like I just read the question wrong so I put the wrong number, or I second-guessed myself. So I won't be, like, super mad at myself because then I'll just be stressed. I stay calm and ask a friend or my teacher for help.

"If she has a difficult time in math or on a test, she just talks it out," says Abby. "Sometimes you can't over-think it, just put a plus sign there."

On top of taking math, I have classes like science and social studies. I really like English and art. In English, we do a lot of reading and writing and journal entries and peer editing and answering the teacher's questions for homework.

In art class sometimes we work with clay. Like right now, I'm making a teapot. My teapot has the love sign and my name spelled out on the side, with the apostrophe on top. And for the handle, I'm going to sculpt myself out of clay.

Music is another one of my favorite classes. This year we studied Mozart and Beethoven and all those guys. It was interesting learning about how they wrote their music. And we watched this one movie about Mozart called *Amadeus*. It was probably one of the best old-time movies I've ever seen.

After school ends, I have a period of waiting till sports practice starts. So if I have a lot of homework, I might do some of it. I also do homework during extra help, which is like study hall.

When I practice sports, I work hard to master the fundamentals. Take basketball. Coach Brady, my basketball coach at Springside, teaches us that basketball is all about math. When you're shooting from the free-throw line, the backboard runs at a ninety-degree angle from the ball when you shoot it.

"In order to throw a successful bounce pass, you have to bounce the ball two-thirds of the way between you and the person receiving the ball," says Coach Brady. "So take that distance between the two of you, divide it by three, bounce the ball on the two-thirds part, and you will be successful."

If you want to score a layup, the easiest way is to come in to the backboard at a forty-five-degree angle.

Basketball workouts make me tired, and sometimes my legs hurt. After practice is over, I get on the bus, and we wind our way back through the city again.

"Sometimes on the five o'clock bus home with her, I would say, 'Mo'ne, do you wanna stop sports? Are you tired? When do you breathe?'" says Nahla. "It just seemed impossible to me to do all that, but here's a girl that does it so easily and you can tell that she loves it."

Two hours later the bus drops me off at my house.

"Mo'ne is the first one on the bus in the morning and

the last one off at night," says Qu'ran.

When I get home I eat and do some more homework, then go over to Anderson to practice.

Between games, we work very hard on learning what Coach calls the fundamentals—the basic skills that each sport is based upon.

In basketball, Coach sets up bright orange cones in the gym and we zigzag through them, dribbling the ball with our right hand first. When we reach the end of the cones, we spin around. Then we zigzag through the cones, dribbling the ball with our left hand. In soccer, it's sort of the same thing, but you dribble with your feet. So we dribble around the cones, then stop the ball and spin around so the ball rolls with us. Then we practice passing with our right foot, then passing with our left.

In baseball, we stand in front of the mirror in the batting cage with our feet planted wide, so that the V of our legs makes a triangle with the floor. We pick up the bat, then pull our arms straight back so that our front elbows are stretched but flexed in what we call the "rubber-band pose," and we put our hands near our back shoulder. Our head is on one side of our arm and our face on the other. Then we practice our swing.

I kept practicing my pitching, and it got better and better. When you're pitching, your goal is simple: to get the batter out. You can do that a lot of ways. One way is to make the batter swing and miss. To make that happen you can keep the batter off balance by mixing up your pitches.

The main pitch is a fastball. To throw one, you grip the ball with your pointer and middle fingers a natural width apart, but perpendicular across the seams of the ball. The seams are the red stitches around the ball, where the ball, which is made of leather, is sewn together. (The inside of a ball is made of cork or rubber and has so much string wrapped around it that if you opened it and stretched it, it could reach almost a mile.) Your thumb goes underneath the ball across the opposite seam. Then you just reach back and let it rip.

You can do a lot with a basic fastball. One way you make the batter swing is to change where you throw the ball—down low by their knees, up high by their chest, close to their body, or far away.

Another way to make the batter miss is to change how you throw the ball. A fastball can go straight, sink, or give the optical illusion that it's rising or moving slow. When you throw a good hard fastball, we say that you're throwing a "heater" or "bringing the heat."

I also learned how to throw a curveball—but not until I was twelve, because it's harder to do. To throw a curveball, you hold your pointer and middle fingers close together on top of or parallel to a seam with your thumb across the opposite seam. That gives the ball a lot of top-spin, which makes it curve downward as it gets close to the plate. Because you throw a curveball a lot slower than a fastball, you can really throw a batter off if he's expecting a fastball but you throw him a curve. Then there's a "dirty curve," which dives but also curves toward the inside or outside edge of the plate. Dirty curves are nasty and hard to hit.

Then there's a changeup, which I'm still learning to throw. When you're the batter, it looks a lot like a fastball, but it comes a lot slower. You can't tell that it's coming slower until it's really close to the plate. By then you may already have swung the bat and missed.

Strike one!

Another way to get a batter out is to throw the ball in the strike zone—an imaginary rectangle over home plate that is as wide as the plate and as long as the distance between the batter's armpits and knees—but to fool the batter into not swinging. *Strike two!*

Every now and then, I also throw a quick pitch—when I don't take as long as I usually do to throw it. A quick pitch catches a batter off guard and messes up their rhythm.

Strike three!

Another way to get a batter out is to make them hit the ball to one of the other players—in baseball we call them fielders—so that the players catch it on the fly, in the air, before it touches the ground. Or the batter can hit the ball to a fielder, who picks it up off the ground so they can throw the batter or another runner out.

But you have to practice. To get better I throw thousands of pitches in the pitching cage.

"Even if we don't go there as part of our practice, every day she goes in there to perfect her craft," says Zion.

When I'm done practicing sports, usually I go home, take my shower, and get ready for the next day.

"Mo'ne does her homework in the kitchen between ten o'clock and one in the morning," says Qu'ran. "She's drinking Canada Dry ginger ale and on her computer listening to 'Fancy' by Iggy Azalea, and she listens to Fifth Harmony."

The next day I do it all over again. That's the other thing about hard work—you have to really like what you're doing because you're going to do it A LOT. But even if you don't always enjoy what you're doing, if you do it with friends they can help make it fun.

Studying and perfecting my craft—Jackie Robinson did it. And Marian Anderson, she did it also. Even though her family was poor and her church came together to help her pay for voice lessons, she became great. In 1939, First Lady Eleanor Roosevelt invited her to sing at the Lincoln Memorial before seventy-five thousand people. In 1955, she became the first black woman allowed to sing at the Metropolitan Opera House in New York City. And John F. Kennedy invited her to sing the national anthem when he became president. Maybe when Marian Anderson was a girl she had big dreams like me.

CHAPTER 8
BEING COMMITTED

BY THE TIME I WAS TEN, THE MONARCHS WERE GETTING really good at all three sports, and I was becoming a really good basketball player. Around Philly, people in youth basketball were starting to know my name.

In one game against Frankford Recreation Center, one of my moves ended up on YouTube after a kid on their team hit a three-pointer on us.

We inbounded the ball, and I slowly walked up the court dribbling. In basketball, I play the point guard position. The point guard in basketball is like the quarterback in football. We get the plays from the coach, and then we run the offense.

Coach Steve gave us the signal for everyone to spread out and for me to drive to the basket. When I reached the top of the key, I started the play. The boy who had hit the three-pointer was guarding me. I faked him like I was going in one direction, then crossed the ball over to the other hand and dribbled in the opposite direction. He fell on his butt. While he was lying on the ground, I drove up under the basket to make them think that I was going to shoot a layup. But then I passed off to Nasir and he scored from the corner. I didn't know it till later, but somebody was videotaping the game. That was my first "ankle-breaker," the slang for a play where you fake out an opponent and he stumbles. We won the game.

That year, 2011, turned out to be a big year for us. The Monarchs won the championship in four different sports—indoor soccer, outdoor soccer, basketball, and baseball—even though we were playing in the ten-and-under league.

The basketball championship was against Somerton at Vogt Recreation Center in the northeast part of Philadelphia. We were down by just one point with sixteen seconds left, and then Scott came through with a free throw to tie it and send us to overtime. We won in the second overtime.

That same day we had an indoor soccer championship against Port Richmond. The kids from Port Richmond were old rivals. The first time we played them, we finished in a tie. The next year, the game went to double overtime. The soccer championship was scheduled so close to the basketball championship that we didn't even get to stay for the awards ceremony.

"Oh my goodness, we were running from the basketball championship to the soccer championship, and they were changing their clothes in the car," my mom says. "It was hectic!"

Indoor soccer is different from outdoor soccer. For one thing, there is no out of bounds—the ball can go in the stands and bounce back on the floor and you can still play it.

In the last period of this game, the Monarchs were down by a goal. Then on one play, the ball bounced up into the bleachers, and someone batted it right back onto the court. It went straight to Scott, who was standing at midcourt. Scott kicked the ball with his left foot while it was still in the air, and scored! No one could believe he'd done that. You might see that kind of play in the World Cup, but for anybody else, it's super hard to do.

Scott's shot tied the game. After that, we played two overtimes, but the game was still tied so we went into a shoot-out. Scott was the first shooter, and his shot hit the crossbar. It was so close! Then it was Port Richmond's turn to kick. They missed.

The game kept going back and forth after that. Their player would kick and miss, and we would kick and miss.

Everyone sat nervously on the sidelines for several rounds, waiting while each player took their shot.

Then Port Richmond scored. All of a sudden, we were down by one.

It was my turn to kick. If I missed it, we were going to lose.

I ran onto the floor and stared at the goal. Then I took my approach and kicked it into the left-hand corner. The score was even again.

The next Port Richmond player missed his shot. Then on the ninth shot of the shootout Myles came up and ripped it. Myles kicked it high and to the upper left.

Scooooooore!

The whole place went kind of crazy.

After the game ended we had to run out the door. We were late to a preseason baseball game.

Our baseball game was at Anderson against the Philly Bobcats, a new team that had been started at the Taney Baseball League at Markward Playground. We beat them that day, too. It was pretty much a blowout.

What a really amazing day!

....

Around the Fourth of July of that year we had a great experience when we went to Rehoboth Beach, Delaware, for the Sports at the Beach baseball tournament. We played three teams that day, in the quarterfinals, the semifinals, and then the championships. We blew out this team called the Hurricanes. Then we played this team called the Revolution. They chanted the word *revolution* over and over throughout the game.

I pitched inning after inning, without them scoring any runs and getting only two hits.

It was my first shutout.

"That was the year that Roy Halladay was pitching real well," Scott says, "so we started calling her Mo Halladay."

We didn't win the championship that day. We lost to the CB Stars from New York. But it felt really good to be pitching so well.

But by the end of the summer, all the running around from game to game to game started to wear me down, especially when it came to baseball.

Basketball was my favorite sport—I just like the whole game and that it's fast-paced. I didn't really like baseball that much at all. Especially when we were younger and still learning how to play, it seemed slow and kind of boring. Plus we played so many games that it took up the whole summer.

That was the summer that my mom took the family to all the water parks in the Philadelphia area.

They went to Six Flags Great Adventure, Dorney Park, Hersheypark, Sesame Place, and Clementon Park, but I didn't go to any of them.

Whenever my mom tried to pick a day that I could go, I had a baseball tournament. I would be standing on a scorching-hot field while Qu'ran was going down the Python Plummet, the Demon Drop, and the Nitro. Then I would hear all my siblings, friends, and cousins tell stories about how much fun they had.

Coach scheduled so many games that we almost never had free weekends. It was too much. That fall I thought a lot about quitting.

But my teammates didn't want me to leave. They were like, "Just play one more year and see how you like it." We were about to move up from the small field that nine- and ten-year-olds play on to the sixty-by-ninety-foot field for older kids. Maybe on a bigger field things would change, they said.

But I had already been complaining to my mom.

"It wouldn't be right to quit," my mother told me. "You've made a commitment to be a Monarch, and your coach and teammates are counting on you."

My mom let me miss a couple of games that summer, but only if they were against a team that we would beat by a lot. We would always make sure to tell Coach Steve if I wasn't going to make it. Coach Steve isn't a yeller, but the one time he would yell at kids was if they didn't tell him that they couldn't come and just didn't show up to a game.

Someone told Coach Steve what was on my mind.

"I heard it from Robin, who heard it from Keisha," Coach says. A lot of people, they call my mom Keisha. "I didn't press it because I didn't wanna get into a big conversation and give her an out. I kind of wanted to say, 'You're playing and that's it,' and just keep going until she said she didn't wanna play anymore. So my position was, 'We need you and you're already committed to this season.' And thank god she stayed with it."

The Monarchs are big on being accountable. If you say you're gonna do something, your teammates should be able to count on you.

Plus, I knew that Coach was already planning a barnstorming tour. The more I learned about it, the more I wanted to go.

CHAPTER 9
GOING BARNSTORMING

IN JULY 2012, WHEN I WAS ELEVEN YEARS OLD, COACH STEVE took the Monarchs on a barnstorming tour. It was the sixty-fifth anniversary of Jackie Robinson integrating the major leagues, and the MLB All-Star Game was going to be held in Kansas City. Kansas City is where the Kansas City Monarchs used to play. It is also the home of the Negro Leagues Baseball Museum. Coach thought that the Anderson Monarchs could pay tribute to Jackie Robinson by playing baseball with teams all around the country, and that we could go to the All-Star Game and see the National Baseball Hall of Fame.

This wasn't Coach Steve's first barnstorming tour. In

1997—four years before I was born—he organized a trip with his very first Anderson Monarchs team to mark the fiftieth year that Jackie Robinson integrated baseball. That was the same year that the league retired his number. In every baseball stadium in the country, you will see Jackie Robinson's jersey number, forty-two.

To show people that kids of different races could develop friendships, in 1997 Coach put together a team of five white kids, five black kids, and five Latino kids from all over Philadelphia. In 2004, when they were thirteen, he took them barnstorming to twenty cities. Along the way they covered 4,500 miles. Now he wanted to barnstorm with us, but everyone had to do a lot to make that happen.

First, we had to do some homework to get us ready for the tour. Every Friday for about twenty weeks, Coach had us watch episodes of the documentary *Baseball* by Ken Burns.

We learned a lot about the history of the sport, and more about the Negro Leagues and African American players who helped to make the game—players like Mamie "Peanut" Johnson, the first woman to pitch in the Negro Leagues. I was surprised and thought it was kind of cool that there had been a woman pitcher in the Negro Leagues.

We also had to raise money to go on the trip. Well,

Coach Steve raised most of it, but he also made us do a lot of work.

"Each parent had to sell one hundred raffle tickets for five dollars each," my mom remembers. "If we didn't sell the raffle tickets, we were responsible for five hundred dollars. I sold seven hundred dollars' worth of raffle tickets and we sold dinners at Anderson. We raised a lot of money."

Enough for us to be gone for three weeks and visit twenty different cities.

Right before we left, we met Matt Kemp of the Los Angeles Dodgers, an African American All-Star outfielder and Gold Glove and Silver Slugger award winner, at a Phillies game two days before we started the tour. He played for the same team as Jackie Robinson! The Brooklyn Dodgers moved to Los Angeles about ten years after Jackie Robinson broke the color barrier, but they still celebrate Jackie Robinson's legacy. Several African American players learned that the Anderson Monarchs were going to go barnstorming and wanted to meet us.

Coach Steve also gave all of us navy blue wristbands that said *Empathy, Integrity, Leadership, and Accountability*, four of the character traits that he teaches us. Any time we needed a reminder of who we were, we were supposed to look at our wristbands.

To make the trip as real as possible, Coach found an old-fashioned bus from 1947. Our bus was black and white and said *Anderson Monarchs Baseball Club* across the top of it. The night before we left, I found out that we were going to take that old bus. At first I thought the trip would be bad because the bus didn't have any air-conditioning, but it ended up being a lot of fun because, mostly, the weather was super nice, and we got to see a lot of cities. Coach Steve had set up games with any team that would play us.

Our first stop was Secaucus, New Jersey, right outside of New York City. When we got off the bus we went to the MLB Network. We got to go into the studio that they broadcast from, which was really nice. The studio is called Studio 42, which was Jackie Robinson's number, and was set up to look like a baseball field—it was like a little Wiffle ball field. There was fake grass, a pitcher's mound and base paths made of dirt-brown artificial turf, real bases, a dugout, Gatorade bottles, a bat rack, and helmets from every team. They even had a replica of Jackie Robinson's uniform, and a plaque to honor him hanging in their broadcast stadium. On the outfield walls, you could see the scores of every major league game that was being played. They told us that the field was so real that we could have played Wiffle ball on it if they hadn't been filming.

After we left the studio we drove up to Harlem for our first game. Everywhere we went, we exchanged gift bags with little presents like Philadelphia souvenirs and Jackie Robinson Hall of Fame cards that we gave to kids on opposing teams. We also gave away these really cool pins Coach had made just for the barnstorming tour. They were navy, white, and gold, and were round like a baseball with baseball thread around the edges, our barnstorming bus blazing through the middle, and the skyline of Philadelphia right behind the bus. Then we played a game. The other team was really nice, so after the game we ended up talking to them for a little bit.

We also visited Jackie Robinson's grave. Jackie Robinson is buried in Cypress Hills cemetery in Brooklyn, New York. It is very green and has a lot of trees. His tombstone is kind of tall—it comes about to a man's chest—and it is curved at the top. On it is a saying: "A life is not important except in the impact it has on other lives."

That saying is also on the back of the bus we sometimes take to games. Coach talks about it all the time.

The things that Jackie Robinson did impacted a lot of African American baseball players in the past, and players of all races today. When I first read the saying, I didn't know that pretty soon I would have the ability to impact other people also.

At the bottom of his tombstone, there was this patch

of dirt that was filled with flowers and baseballs that people had written letters to him on. All of us wrote a little note or a question for him, then we lined our baseballs up in a row. I can't remember what I wrote now.

From New York, we hopped back on the bus and drove to Pittsburgh, which took seven hours. It was the longest ride of the entire trip, and the fact that we drove through Times Square before we left New York made it longer. While we were riding, we laughed, joked around, listened to music, played Uno and BS—well, we called it "Nike and Adidas" so we didn't use any bad words— made up a rap song, and slept. We played all these games because no electronics were allowed on the trip. Coach, he says I use electronics too much. Sometimes he calls me "Screen Face Davis."

When we got to Pittsburgh, we went to the Josh Gibson Foundation. Josh Gibson was one of the greatest home-run hitters of all time. Many people used to call him the black Babe Ruth. After he died, his family started an organization to help children in Pittsburgh reach their potential. The next day we played a game against a team that Josh Gibson's great-grandson coached.

We also walked over the Allegheny River on the Roberto Clemente Bridge. Roberto Clemente was a Puerto Rican baseball player who played for the Pittsburgh Pirates. He was the National League MVP once, made the National League All-Star team twelve times, was the National League batting champion four times, and won the Gold Glove award for being the best fielder twelve times. Roberto Clemente was killed in an airplane crash trying to help people in Nicaragua after an earthquake. After he died, he became the first Latino player to be inducted into the National Baseball Hall of Fame.

When we were standing on the bridge, we could see downtown Pittsburgh on one side and PNC Park, where the Pirates play, on the other. Then we went to a Pittsburgh Pirates game with some of the kids from the Josh Gibson team. The Pirates' stadium was probably one of the best stadiums we went to. One of the cool things about it is that they had these bushes in the back with the word *Pirates* spelled out on them. Also, we got to meet Josh Harrison, who plays third base for the Pirates.

From Pittsburgh, we went to Cleveland. In Cleveland, we were supposed to meet the Los Angeles Angels. But it was raining, so the Angels' batting practice was canceled. But some of the pitchers for the Cleveland Indians—Tony Sipp, Justin Masterson, and Joe Smith—came out on the field with the catcher, Carlos Santana. They met us and said, "Let's do some stretching," so we ran out to center field and did some stationary stretches with them. Some of the players invited us to play catch. Then one of the pitchers wanted to see us run around the bases, then point to where we were going to hit a home run and try to hit it there. Then we went into the dugout with them.

From Cleveland, we went to Detroit. I remember that Detroit was super, super hot, and we were stuck in traffic on a bus with no air-conditioning. The bus driver gave us trivia questions.

After we played in Detroit, we went to Chicago.

In Chicago we went to this big pizza restaurant, which I remember because pizza is my favorite food.

After Chicago, we traveled to Dyersville, Iowa, to have batting practice on the "field of dreams" from the movie. It was an open field, so there were a lot of people fulfilling their dream of playing there. Two little boys were taking batting practice. So we threw the ball around and took a picture with them.

From there, we went to Cedar Rapids. It was raining when we got there. The team we were going to play, the Reds, greeted us when we got off the bus. We took pictures together, had a ceremony, and ate hot dogs and hamburgers with each other, then sat in the bleachers and talked. Then they got on the bus and rode with us to a minor league game. When we got there, the announcer introduced us on the field. Then both teams hung out together, talking to each other on this big patch of grass.

When the game was over, the kids got back on the

bus with us. Then we gave each other gift bags. They gave us a hat and a cup holder.

The next day the Reds handed us our first loss on our trip. The kids on their team were thirteen and fourteen years old, so they were about two years older than us—but we only lost by one run. That was a nice game.

We made our way to Kansas City next, which was a lot of fun. Along the way, all of us had been buying baseball cards, and we pretended that we managed teams and made our own lineups.

When we got to Kansas City, we went to the Royals' FanFest and the All-Star Legends and Celebrity Softball Game. At FanFest, fans could try out baseball equipment, play baseball video games, get a baseball card with their picture on it, sit in a dugout, and do a whole lot of other fun stuff. At the Celebrity Softball Game, a lot of stars played softball. That year, some stars from the TV shows *Mad Men*, *Glee*, and *Desperate Housewives* played, along with a bunch of reality show stars. USA Softball's Olympic Gold Medalist hurler Jennie Finch was one of the pitchers.

We watched the Home Run Derby. Matt Kemp did pretty well that year, but Prince Fielder won.

We also went to the Negro Leagues Baseball Museum. At the Negro Leagues Museum you can find out anything you want to know about the Negro League players. They have old uniforms, players' bats and baseballs and other memorabilia, and lectures and educational programs. You see things like old chairs marked *Colored* because during segregation in parts of this country, white people didn't let African American players sit in the same chairs as they did.

While we were there, we talked to a man who actually knew Jackie Robinson and wrote him a lot of letters. He even read one of his letters to us.

Then we ran into Matt Kemp again. He was at the museum to accept an award.

From Kansas City we went to Columbia, and then St. Louis. Then on to Louisville, Kentucky, where we visited the Louisville Slugger Museum and Factory, where they make the famous Louisville Slugger bat.

From there we went to Indianapolis, Indiana; and then Cincinnati and South Point, Ohio.

One thing about the barnstorming tour was that we were only allowed to call home once a week. Squirt says that I didn't call until the fifteenth day and I only called because I needed more money.

"Mo'ne's very independent," my mom says. "I guess she gets that from me."

From South Point, we drove on to Washington, DC.

When we were in Washington, I met Miss Mamie

"Peanut" Johnson in person. Meeting Miss Mamie Johnson was really cool. Coach had made me read a book about her before I met her. I found out that she even played with Hammerin' Hank Aaron on the same Negro League team, the Indianapolis Clowns. Hank Aaron is an African American outfielder, who went on to play in the MLB for the Milwaukee Braves, a team that later moved to Atlanta. In 1973 he became the first player to beat Babe Ruth's home run record.

Miss Mamie was really energized to meet me, and gave me good advice.

"Don't ever throw the ball down the heart of the plate," she told me. "Always put it to the inside or the outside. And if you put it close to the player, put it right underneath his armpits."

She told me that she started playing baseball when she was my age, and that she had a lot of fun striking out the guys.

"All you've got to do is strike them all out," she told me. Then she told a photographer something I'd never thought of before: "I predict she's gonna be the first lady in the major leagues."

Miss Mamie even came to our game—I was pitching that day! And she likes to yell. I could hear her while I was pitching, saying, "Follow through, Mo!" and "Take your time, baby!" I felt really inspired. I think I pitched five and two-thirds innings that game, and the Monarchs won 6–0.

So the rest of the time during the tour, my teammates and some of our fans started telling me to "Take your time, baby!"

Later that year, when I went back to school, I made this sculpture in art class that I called *Peanut and Me*. It has two white circles of clay, like baseballs, with a big one on the bottom and a little one on top. She was the big circle, and the little one standing on her shoulders was me.

After the game, we went to the Lincoln Memorial, a huge white building with all these columns around it, like a Greek temple, built to honor Abraham Lincoln, the president who ended slavery. The weather was super hot and we had to walk up a lot of steps to get to the top. But when you reach it, you see a big statue of President Lincoln, and you can look down across to the Washington Monument. I remembered that this was the place where Marian Anderson sang in front of all those people. I imagined that it must have been really nerve-racking. A photographer took pictures of us while we were there. A couple of the kids took a walk around the monument, but there were so many people there that we had to look for them before we left.

Then we went to the Martin Luther King, Jr. Memorial. I really liked how the statue was sculpted to make it look like he was looking down over us. Then we walked along the black granite wall that is filled with Dr. King's sayings, and tried to read all the quotes that we could.

"The ultimate measure of a man is not where he stands in moments of comfort and convenience, but where he stands at times of challenge and controversy."

My life hasn't always been the most convenient or comfortable, but I've tried to live up to the challenge.

After Washington, we went to Baltimore, where we wound up the barnstorming tour with a win. We finished with a 16–2 record. We were exhausted, darkly suntanned, and had been exposed to a whole new world.

After we left Baltimore, we came home to Philly for a day or two, then we went right up to Cooperstown, New York, home of the National Baseball Hall of Fame. When we got there, we went to the ceremony they have every year, where they induct great retired players into the Hall of Fame.

I remember that it was so, so hot and we were wearing

our uniforms and had our hats on. They gave everyone a bottle of water, but we all finished ours because it was so super hot.

Barry Larkin, who played shortstop for the Cincinnati Reds, and Ron Santo, who played third base for the Chicago Cubs, were inducted into the Hall of Fame that year.

Later that day, I went to a CVS drugstore. Just as we were walking in, Barry Larkin was walking out. He gave us all a little card that had the Hall of Fame plaque and something written about him on it, and signed it.

That weekend we also played a team from Oneonta, New York. I was batting fourth, which was different for me—I usually batted second.

The first pitch I swung at and missed. *Strike one!* The next pitch was low, but I got a good cut at it and connected. I hit a line drive. But that line drive kept going and going and going—I hit it out of the park. It was my first home run! And nobody was more surprised than me. I was super, super glad that I hadn't quit baseball.

It was a lot of hard work and a lot of time on the road. But it was also a lot of fun. I was seeing the country with my friends, getting to play baseball, and learning a lot about the role African Americans played in baseball history, as well as learning more about Marian Anderson and Martin Luther King.

....

That fall a new kid, Zion, joined our team.

"The first time I came to practice, I was sitting alone and the team was all together, and she came over and introduced herself and then brought me to the rest of the team," Zion says.

Zion always prays before our games. He goes to the same school as Scott, so he stays overnight at Coach Steve's a lot, too, and he and I became very good friends.

Zion is very funny. One time Scott was in the kitchen, and Zion called Scott's name from another part of the house, and then turned out the lights. I froze because I'm afraid of the dark. Scott walked really slowly through the dining room, the living room, and even looked in the bathroom, knowing that Zion was going to jump out and scare him. But he couldn't find Zion. I knew where Zion was, but I wasn't telling. When Scott walked back into the bathroom, he saw Zion standing there pressed up flat against the wall, holding a baseball bat over his head. Zion yelled "Woo!" and scared everyone.

CHAPTER 10

LET IT SHINE

THE KID TOOK ONE STEP OFF OF FIRST BASE, THEN HE crouched down and took two more steps sideways— shuffle, shuffle. He turned his head back toward first base and looked at his coach. Then he looked back toward the field and took one more shuffle-step away from the bag.

I was standing on the mound, facing third, with my hand in my mitt, getting my grip for my next pitch. It was the spring of 2013, and we were playing a team from New Jersey on our home field at Anderson.

I had the runner in my peripheral vision, but I didn't know that he was following the same pattern every time he took his lead. Fortunately, Scott saw it. Scott sees everything, and by now, we hardly needed to say any words to know what the other was thinking.

I was starting to get good at pick-off plays—quick throws to catch runners who stray too far off a base while one of their teammates is at bat. Sometimes, when I was playing shortstop, I'd give a secret signal to Scott, who usually played catcher, to tell him I thought we could pick a kid off. Our pitcher would pitch the ball, and Scott would then rifle it to me. I'd tag the runner.

Out!

Before I started my movement to pitch, Scott called a time-out.

"I walked out to the mound," says Scott. "I went, 'Mo, the kid who's on first base? After his second step off, he looks back to the base every single time.'"

Then Scott turned around and walked back to home plate.

I set up to throw my next pitch, and out of the corner of my eye, I saw the pattern that Scott was talking about. Scott signaled a fastball, and I threw it.

"She pitched once, just like I hadn't told her anything," Scott says.

Then Scott threw the ball back to me like normal and I set up for the next pitch.

"She sets, and the kid goes shuffle, shuffle, and, right when he looks back, Mo'ne fires to the first baseman,"

Scott says. "She did it without me even saying a word. Most kids would have been like, 'What do you mean?' when I went to the mound. The kid she picked off didn't even know what happened."

The Monarchs had been playing together long enough that we didn't even need to speak to each other and were able to make playing look easy.

But the thing about sports is that you have your ups and downs and you have to keep playing through. Sometimes things go your way, and sometimes things don't. That's all part of the game.

Coach Steve, he tells us to always stay classy. Even if you win or lose, always have the same expression on your face, and don't let the other team know that you're mad about anything.

That June, we went to the tournament at the Cooperstown All Star Village, where teams like ours play other teams from around the whole country. We did pretty well that year—we came in fifth. And we got to meet kids from all across the country.

Zion likes to talk to people, so he puts himself out there with other teams and helps us meet a lot of new kids. We got really close to two teams at that tournament: the Minnesota Storm and the Sacramento Hitmen.

We played the Hitmen in the quarterfinals and beat them. After the game, we exchanged hats and undershirts—the team T-shirts that we wear under our uniforms—like we normally do with kids from other teams. We also exchanged Instagram names and phone numbers.

There was another team from Minnesota. We thought they liked all of us, but they only liked Sami. That's just how it is sometimes—everyone loves Sami. Sami is super, super social. He came in really handy when we met a team from the Dominican Republic. In case you don't know, Dominicans are big in Major League Baseball.

Not all of the team from the DR spoke English. Fortunately, Demetrius takes Spanish classes, so he knew what they were saying. There was one kid on the team who was super nice, and who spoke a little English. We were trying to teach him English, and he was trying to teach us Spanish.

One day, the Dominican kids played a big joke on us and made something that they called Dominican soda. Really they just took a bunch of fountain drinks and mixed them together, and put salt and pepper in them, and tried to get someone to drink it.

"You wanna try this?" they'd ask some of the kids on our team. "It's soda we brought with us from the Dominican Republic."

"We don't trust the look on your face," people would tell them. "No way!"

Tamir wasn't there when they started the joke, so he didn't know he was getting pranked. He drank it and his face scrunched up. Everybody laughed. Laughing is the same in every language.

Then Zion came around and the Dominican kids handed him some.

"What is this?" he said when he looked in the cup and smelled it.

He didn't fall for the joke.

Most of the time when we play in baseball tournaments, the teams trade hats, T-shirts, and pins with each other. We had our barnstorming pins and everybody wanted one.

The Dominican kids didn't have pins to trade, but they did have necklaces in red, white, and blue—the colors of the Dominican Republic's flag—and bracelets with their flag on it.

Their necklaces were really cool—everybody wanted one. They were like twisted rope, and had a DR flag on them. They stayed on with a little baseball that you slipped through a circle with a knot. But they didn't have a lot of them.

"We'll trade you these pins for them?" we asked with our fingers crossed. "No one has a pin like this at this tournament but us. We'll trade you. . . ."

At first, they weren't giving their bracelets and necklaces out. But after the final game, all of us kids were standing on the hill, talking and laughing, and trading pins and undershirts and hats. One of the best things about playing sports is that you have a lot of fun and make a lot of friends from all over the country and even around the world.

That was the same year that I had my worst day as a pitcher. During the fall league championship game, we were playing one of the best teams, and we were tied with them for first place. The weather was cloudy and cold, and I was pitching. I don't like to pitch in the cold because my hands get cold and feel hard, and I can't grip the ball right. I was not doing well. I walked so many people that it wasn't even funny. Needless to say, we were losing. Those are the kinds of days when you really need your teammates to cheer you up. We were sitting in the dugout, and the Monarchs were at bat. The sun had started to come out from behind the clouds a little bit.

"This little light of mine, I'm gonna let it shine. . . ." Myles started singing.

What?!

"I'm gonna let it shine, I'm gonna let it shine. . . ."

Myles and his singing just came out of nowhere. It

was so random that we all started laughing.

"Let it shine, let it shine, let it shine. . . ."

But his singing and laughing seemed to pick us up. Suddenly we started coming back from behind.

"Keep singing, keep singing," we kept telling Myles.

We won the fall championship!

Myles would just start singing sometimes, and his singing became like good luck to us. Another day when we were down, we told Myles, "Sing while you're batting!"

He started singing that song on his way up to the plate. We thought it was funny. We could even see his lips moving while he was standing at the plate and batting. For some reason, Myles kept singing and singing. He was an inspiration to us, and next thing we knew, he had hit a home run. Sweet!

We always laughed and had fun with each other and kept each other in a good mood.

That year, I got a lot better in basketball also. Even though my goal as the point guard is to help my teammates to score, sometimes Coach Brady asks me to help.

"Okay, Mo, now it's time," she tells me. "We need you to score some points."

"Okay, Coach."

When a coach asks a point guard to score, most of the time they mean that we should run some fast breaks.

So I turn on the gas, but only as hard as I have to for us to get where Coach Brady wants us.

"She fakes people out; she does it under her legs and behind her back," says Destiny.

"One game we were yelling and calling her Mo'ne, Mo'zart, Mo'ney, Money Mo', Mo' Easy," says Nahla. "If you look in her eyes, you just see the determination to win."

It's always important to listen to the coach and be thoughtful about the other members of your team. When we catch back up, Coach will say, "Let's see who else can contribute to the game." Then I go back to the point guard's main role of setting my teammates up to score.

But every game is not a success. The next month my team played Abington. Coach asked me to score some points, and I did—I scored thirty-four of our team's forty-six points. But when the game was on the line, I let my team down. I missed five out of five free throws in the fourth quarter. The game ended in a tie, and it was all my fault. Normally I make 90 percent of my free throws. We would have won if I had made even one of them.

"Normally the game's over, that's it; win, lose, or whatever, she says, 'That was fun, we did our best,' and it's over," Coach Brady says. "This one she was visibly upset. For a moment she hung her head. But if you don't know her well enough, you wouldn't know it."

One of the things that I thought was really cool that year was that at the end of the school year, I won the seventh grade advisors' award. I didn't know that the teachers, they watch your every step. So they pick certain things up about you like how well you manage your work and stay close to your friends. The award is for a girl who has a great work ethic, calm determination, and great tenacity in everything she does and inspires others to do their best work. I try very hard to be that girl.

CHAPTER 11
THE CHANCE TO COMPETE

AFTER ALL THE HARD WORK, SACRIFICE, AND DEDICATION, the summer of 2014, when I turned thirteen years old, was the best year of my young life.

That April baseball season started off with a bang.

On a day that was a little chilly but kind of warm, I hit a home run on my very first at bat. The next day, I hit another home run. We were winning, and the bases were loaded, and the ball faded right toward the foul line but stayed fair, and this time it made it over the wall. It was my very first grand slam.

For the next five weeks, I hit a home run every week. I don't know how I did it. I think I retired from the twelve-year-olds' team tied with Zion for the most grand slams—that year I hit two.

My pitches were humming also. It was kind of like I had found this zone.

"Physically she had refined her game and had command of her pitches," Coach Steve says. "There are a lot of kids who throw harder, but none of them pitch."

But I was throwing pretty hard. One day, Coach Steve brought a radar gun to practice and clocked one of my pitches at sixty-seven miles per hour. Wow! I wasn't even throwing hard that day.

At the same time, we still played in the Tri-State Elite Baseball League and in weekend tournaments. After school let out in June, we played in the Cooperstown All Star Village tournament again, a thirty-two-team national tournament against teams from all across the country.

We went in as one of the tournament's underdogs. Some of the other teams were the kind that go out every year to try to recruit the best players they can find. They do whatever it takes to win. Sometimes the kids don't even know each other. They just fly in and out and don't see each other in between. Their only goal is to win. That's about the opposite of the Monarchs, where we see each other almost every day, and everyone plays baseball, basketball, and soccer, even if it's not their best or favorite sport.

Our first game out, we beat the San Carlos Stingers on the Green Monster, the name of one of the fields that has a twenty-feet-high outfield fence. Then we beat another California team or two and even a Texas team. We proved to ourselves that we could compete with any team in the country.

It was a double-elimination tournament—lose twice and you're out. We came out of the winner's bracket with a 5–1 record.

"We went straight from the bottom team to the powerhouse of the tournament," Scott remembers.

Between games, we lived in the All Star Village together. Our team stayed in the Jackie Robinson bunkhouse. The team right across from us was the Orinda Falcons, from California. We talked to them a lot, and their parents were super nice—they went to McDonald's and brought us back french fries. We traded pins and undershirts with them and all the other kids. By the end of the week, we knew everybody.

At that Cooperstown tournament, we probably had our best-ever day. We played three games in a single day. We won our first two—we beat Top Prospects from Illinois. Then we played the Delta Dawgs from California, another really good team.

"Mo threw a forty-eight-pitch complete game," Scott

says. "They called it after five innings because of the ten-run rule."

The ten-run rule is also called the slaughter rule. It means that if a team gets down by ten, they just end the game so they won't get slaughtered.

Our next game up was against Team Mizuno, a powerhouse team from California.

"The team had no chemistry whatsoever," Scott says. "We could hear the kids calling out numbers because they didn't know each other's names."

The crowd was huge that afternoon—it was a big game!

We were down 4–1 going into the top of the sixth inning, the last inning. Our first two batters that inning got on. But then Scott missed a good pitch and flew out to left field.

I was up next. I got down in the count—it was 0–2. But then I got a good look at a pitch.

"Mo hits a line-drive homer straight over the center-field wall, to tie the game," Scott says. "It was crazy! She put us back in it."

Now the game was tied. Jahli was up, and he was hot! He had already hit two homers that game, and five that day.

So Team Mizuno brought in their best pitcher.

Mo'ne Davis, one year old. "Mo'ne cried for about half an hour before taking this picture in Walmart. She was such a crybaby," her mom, Lakeisha, says.

Mo'ne at her older brother, Qu'ran's, fifth birthday party at WOW skating rink.

Mo'ne's second-grade picture at Francis Scott Key Elementary School, right before she transferred to Springside Chestnut Hill Academy and started playing for the Monarchs.

Mo'ne with her mother on her mother's wedding day in May 2011.

Photo courtesy of Steve Bandura

Mo'ne's first season playing basketball for the Anderson Monarchs.

Mo'ne with her younger sister, Mahogany, playing outside.

Mo'ne with former Anderson Monarchs player Demetrius Jennings and Scott Bandura, her teammate and catcher for the Taney Dragons and the Anderson Monarchs, in Anderson Recreation Center in 2012.

Mo'ne's first time playing baseball for the Anderson Monarchs in 2008.

Mo'ne and some of her best friends practicing basketball drills at Germantown Academy.

Mo'ne playing softball for the first time for Springside Chestnut Hill Academy in 2012.

Mo'ne, her sister, Mahogany, and their mother, Lakeisha, posing for a family portrait in 2012.

Mo'ne with her older brother, Qu'ran, and younger brother, Maurice, at Universal Studios in 2010.

Mo'ne on Blue and Gold Day with her friends Destiny, Nahla, and Ama at Springside Chestnut Hill Academy in 2013.

Mo'ne and her best friends Nayyirah and Ruqayyah after winning the championship game for the summer leagues at Smith Playground in 2013.

Mo'ne and her mother goofing around taking selfies on the set of the Spike Lee documentary *Throw Like a Girl*, about Mo'ne's rise to fame, in September 2014.

Mo'ne at Dodger Stadium with Queen Latifah in September 2014.

Mo'ne meets Maya Moore of the Minnesota Lynx in 2014. Maya Moore is her favorite former UConn women's basketball player.

Coach Steve Bandura, Jeff Idelson (president of the National Baseball Hall of Fame and Museum), Mo'ne, and Mamie "Peanut" Johnson in September 2014. Mo'ne donated her shutout jersey to the Baseball Hall of Fame in Cooperstown, New York.

Mo'ne at basketball practice with the Monarchs in 2014.

"He was HUGE," Scott says. "He was throwing total gas!"

Even Jahli had a hard time handling his fastball. He also had a really good curveball.

"He was throwing *really* hard," Jahli says. "I got a piece of him, but I struck out."

Jared had been pitching that game. It was probably the best game he had ever pitched. He was dealing! He intentionally walked the three and four batters, because they were their best hitters, which meant the bases were loaded. But then he reached the pitch limit we had set for him for that day. Coach brought me into the game.

"She had only thrown forty-eight pitches the game before, so she still had a ton of arm left," says Scott. "There were two outs, and a 2–2 count."

So it was the bottom of the sixth inning and the game was mine to win or lose.

I wasn't really nervous about it, because I knew that I could strike the kid out.

I threw a curveball, right down the middle.

Everyone started walking off the field—the Monarchs, the Mizuno kids on the bases, even the batter. But then the umpire called it a ball.

Are you kidding me? I thought. *Okay, let's just get this next one.*

"Are you kidding me?" Coach Steve shouted at the umpire.

"You're gone!" the umpire yelled right back, giving the sign that Coach had been ejected.

Coach never yells, and here he yells once and he's kicked out of the game on the very last pitch? I had never seen Coach kicked out of a game before. But I had to focus on my pitches.

Now there were two outs, bases loaded, three balls and two strikes, and Coach Steve was on the other side of the fence.

I was pretty calm. Scott and I have been doing this for a long time, and we know each other inside and out. Then Scott did something sneaky. While Jared was pitching, Scott had figured out that the runner on second was stealing his signals.

"I noticed it early in the game," Scott says. "They would move their arms up and down when it was a curveball, and they would fix their jerseys when it was a fastball."

So we called a flip—we changed our signals.

"Mo threw a fastball, right down the middle, and the kid froze since the runner who stole my sign had motioned that it was going to be a curveball," says Scott. "It was a strike."

The kid dropped his head, dropped the bat, and turned toward the dugout.

"Ball four!"

What?! I had no idea what the umpire was thinking!

The batter was as shocked as everyone else. So he walked to first, and the runner on third scored.

We lost to Team Mizuno 6–5.

All the Monarchs threw their gloves down in disgust. Everyone in the crowd started jumping up and down and yelling. Everyone was screaming at the umpire. It was just terrible.

Some of us were so upset, we started crying.

"I wasn't there, since I had to work," my mom says. "But my job was watching it live-streamed on GameChanger. They showed how the ball went right down the middle of the plate."

"And we got it on our camera," says Coach Steve. "We had four cameras filming that game."

After the game, one of the other coaches walked up to Coach Steve.

He said, "It was an absolute travesty what they did to your kids."

For the rest of the afternoon, every coach kept coming up to us and telling us we were robbed. Even the coach of Team Mizuno said, "First of all, I should have been the one kicked out. And second of all, both of those pitches were strikes."

If we had won, we would have played the San Diego Stingers, the team that we had beaten earlier that week, in the championship. Too bad for the Stingers, they had no pitchers left for the championship game. They ended up losing 13–10.

After their game was over, we all went to the championship dinner. The Mizuno kids were already sitting down when we got there, so we went over and congratulated them. We were still upset and we still thought the game had been called unfairly. But Coach had taught us to be classy—win or lose. That's what a Monarch does.

In addition to the schedule we play for the Monarchs, some of us also play in an in-house league at the Baseball League at Markward Playground, just a few blocks from my house.

I didn't know about it then, but at the end of the previous season, Coach Steve had had a conversation with Coach Alex Rice, Taney's baseball coach.

We already knew Coach Alex and his son, Jack, both from playing against Taney and from playing in the Taney league. And Coach Steve ran camps and the kids from Taney would come. We pretty much knew all their players. Jack and another Taney kid, Jared, had also become Monarchs.

Well, it turns out that Jack and Jared had this dream of playing in the Little League World Series. When Jack was nine, Coach Alex had taken him to Williamsport to watch the Little League World Series, and Jack started dreaming about playing in it.

Now, most people think all youth baseball teams are Little League teams, but they're not. You have to apply to be included in Little League and to play in their tournament. Originally the Taney league wasn't officially Little League, and the Monarchs weren't a Little League team either. Coach Alex had to apply to Little League headquarters to get their permission to join. So in 2013, Taney qualified as an official Little League team for the very first time. They did really well for just starting out—they made it to the district tournament.

At the end of that year, Coach Alex and Coach Steve were talking about their plans for next season, since it was the last year that we could play on the small-size baseball field. Your last year is a big deal because when the field jumps up to regulation size, it gets a lot harder and a lot of kids start to drop out.

"We're gonna play Little League for one more year,"

Coach Alex had told Coach Steve. "As far-fetched as it is, Jack and Jared still have this dream of getting to Williamsport."

Coach Steve suggested that the rest of the Monarchs join the Taney League.

"We'll have Scott, Mo'ne, Jahli, and Zion play in both leagues, along with Jack, Jared, and Carter, and they'll be eligible to play in the Little League tournament for the Dragons," Coach Steve said.

"Now that's an idea," Coach Alex said.

"Maybe we'll have a really good team come out of that," Coach Steve said.

"Imagine what the story would be if they ever got to Williamsport with a girl pitcher like Mo'ne." Coach Alex laughed.

"Yeah, I know ESPN would do a story on it." Coach Steve smiled.

Coach Steve tells this story about a movie called *Mickey*, written by John Grisham. In it a dad, who's played by Harry Connick Jr., gets into some money trouble with the government after his wife dies and goes on the lam with his son, and sets up a new life and a new identity. But they had a moral dilemma: the kid had just gotten too old to play in Little League, which ends when you're twelve. (Because my birthday is in June, I still make the cutoff, even though I turned thirteen). But the boy's new identity makes him twelve again. It raises a moral question: What would you do? The kid's dad decided to let him play. Well, it turns out that the kid's Little League team was super good. They made it to the championships in Williamsport and the kid's face ended up on the front page of *USA Today*. Back when he watched it, Coach thought, "There's no way a Little League kid would get famous enough to end up on the front page of *USA Today*."

"When I got the email from Coach Steve saying that Mo'ne plays for another team, I didn't think nothin' of it," my mom recalls. "I'm like, 'Okay, well maybe they needed another pitcher.'"

My mom already knew about the Taney league because Qu'ran had played for them.

I played on a team called the Taney Wizards. My Monarch teammates were scattered across all of the Taney teams—the Wizards, the Centaurs, the Minotaurs, the Cyclops, and other teams. Our games were all over downtown Philadelphia.

"There were days when Mo'ne had a doubleheader with Anderson, then had to go to Taney to play a game. She might pitch at Anderson, and don't pitch at Taney. She might pitch at Taney, but not pitch at Anderson," my mom says.

Yep! I was pretty busy. In between all the Taney

games we played our usual games in the Tri-State Elite League.

"They were everywhere—sometimes they were in New Jersey or out of state," my mom says. "It was hard to know where she had to be from day to day."

When I played for the Wizards, sometimes I had to pitch against my teammates on the Monarchs. That was weird, but also fun.

At the end of the Taney league, my team, the Wizards, actually won the entire Taney tournament. In the Taney league, I got to know the five new kids who would eventually be on the Dragons: Eli, Joe, Kai, Tai, and Erik, this great kid who everybody notices is always smiling.

All totaled, seven different Monarchs—Scott, Jahli, Carter, Jared, Jack, Zion, and me—ended up playing on the Taney Dragons. More of the Monarchs would have played, but some of my teammates, they lived too far from Taney to meet the Little League rules about who qualified.

So this was my new team, and the Taney Dragons really wanted to get to Williamsport.

CHAPTER 12
THE ROAD TO WILLIAMSPORT

THE PATH TO THE LITTLE LEAGUE BASEBALL WORLD SERIES IS a long one, and super hard. You have to play in the district championship in your area and win that. Then you have to win sectionals, states, and regionals to even make it. You've gotta be good—and have a lot of good luck.

Since Coach Alex represented Taney, he became the head coach of the Taney Dragons. Coach Steve stepped aside and basically became just another parent. We weren't wearing Anderson Monarch uniforms anymore. Instead, we wore navy blue jerseys that said *Taney* in white letters. I was wearing my normal number eleven.

We started out in the district tournament, which has ten teams in it.

When we won that we advanced to the sectionals. We won the sectional tournament, and we went on to the states. But after the sectionals, we lost Scott and Jahli from our team. Before any of this had happened, their parents had signed them up to go away to a camp in New Hampshire for a month, and it was already paid for. It was one of those kinds of camps where you can't take your cell phone or talk to your parents. They could only write letters.

So all of a sudden, we didn't have our leadoff hitter or number three hitter—or our catcher or second-base player for that matter. The rest of the team ended up moving around, from position to position, and all around the batting lineup. Coach Alex moved me from second to the top of the batting order, and, in between pitching, I mostly played second base.

The states started with a picnic, where we got to meet all the teams that won their sectional tournaments. We advanced through our bracket and eventually made it to the championship. At one point in the championship game, we were down 4–0, but we got it together and came back to take the lead. When we won, we were like, "Oh my god!" There were 370 teams in the state and we were the best out of all of them. Along the way we adopted a theme song, "We Dem Boyz" by Wiz Khalifa.

The state tournament was held in this town called Skippack. Because all the teams were from Pennsylvania, everyone had a lot of family and friends there to cheer them on. This was a double-elimination tournament— you lose twice and you're out.

When we played the team from Warwick, Eli got hit in the head while he was batting and was dizzy and had to come out of the game. Zion told him he was going to hit a home run for him, and he hit a homer to center field with the bases loaded. We won.

We played this team called Collier, from Pittsburgh, three times. The first time, we won 13–10.

The second time we played it was the first game of the championship round. Since we had beaten them earlier, they would have to beat us twice to win the tournament.

The coach's son was pitching that game. He is a lefty—left-handed pitchers are harder to hit off because you don't face them that often. My first time up, he started by throwing a strike. The second pitch, I laid into it and hit a home run. Little did I know, it would be my last home run of the season.

Without Scott and Jahli, we lost 7–2. We were really upset.

Fortunately, we won our other games. Coming out of the winner's bracket, we had to play against Collier again for the championship.

"It was the night before the championship game, and we think, 'We'd have a much better chance of winning with Scott and Jahli,'" says Squirt.

So Coach Steve made a phone call to the camp. Jahli's dad, Jared's dad—he is also one of our coaches—and Squirt were driving up to get Scott and Jahli. The game was at eight the next morning.

So the dads drove up to camp and then back through the night, while Scott and Jahli slept. They got to the field right before the game started.

The Collier team protested the game because they said that Scott and Jahli weren't on our roster.

I was on the mound for the Dragons. It was do-or-die for both teams.

Scott returned to the top of the batting order.

"I got plunked on the first pitch of the game," says Scott. "It was a hard slider, and it hit me in the butt." He took his base.

I was back to batting number two. I hit the ball up the middle, but it bounced off the rubber and the short-stop turned it into a double play.

We were down 4–1 in the fourth inning, but then Jared hit a home run to make it 4–2. In the sixth inning, there were two runners on and two outs. We were on the brink of elimination, but then Zion hit a three-run homer to give us the lead, 5–4.

The game turned into a nail-biter—and I would know, since I was pitching, and biting my nails is the main thing I do when I'm nervous. Jahli's hands were sweating, which is what happens when he's nervous. Scott was really quiet.

The crowd was getting pretty large, and a lot of the kids from other teams had started cheering for us.

Going into the last inning, we were behind. But we loaded the bases, again. And Scott got a hit with the bases loaded, and we went up by two.

But Collier had one more at bat.

In the bottom of the inning, Jahli really came through defensively, even though he had sweaty hands.

The first out was a routine slow ground ball to him. He threw the runner out at first. The second out was a hard grounder, hit to Jahli also. He handled it. Two outs! The next batter hit a short fly ball.

"It blew over my head into shallow right field," says Jahli. "I ran out for it, and caught it. After I caught it, I just kind of held on to it afterward, knowing that we were going to regionals."

The final score was 6–4.

Everyone contributed to our win that day. Jared went

three for three that game, with a single, a double, and a homer. I had an RBI single with the bases loaded. And Zion hit the game-winning home run.

After the game, Scott and Jahli went back up to New Hampshire and Squirt drove me up to the Pocono Mountains, where I had signed up for a basketball camp. The camp was supposed to be two weeks long, but because we were headed to the regional championship, I could only stay for four days. The camp was a competitive camp, and I had already won some awards and trophies. They weren't happy when Squirt came and took me out. I felt really bad when I left.

So the Taney Dragons traveled to Bristol, Connecticut, to play in the Little League Baseball Mid-Atlantic Regional Tournament. Bristol is about twenty miles southwest of the state capital, Hartford. On top of being a place where, back in the olden days, they used to make a lot of clocks, Bristol is the home of ESPN.

We knew that if we won the regionals, we wouldn't be able to go home. When the tournament is over, the winning team leaves straight from there and goes to Williamsport, Pennsylvania, home of the Little League Baseball World Series.

At the regionals, it was the first time there was a lot of security. There were guards around the outside of the compound, and people couldn't get past a certain point, not even our parents. You had to go through a wooden gate, and you couldn't pass unless you had a badge. Only the players and coaches got badges.

Inside, there were teams from Maryland; Delaware; Pennsylvania; Washington, DC; New Jersey; and New York. The New England regionals were being held there at the same time. We played on alternate days. The night we got there, there was a big grand-slam parade and festival down the streets of the city, and we got to meet everybody on the other teams. Scott ended up with this orange ball that turned out to be good luck for us for the rest of the tournament.

The teams stayed in dorms that circled all around the field. The dorms looked like little houses. Each house had the team's name on it. Inside, when you looked to the right, was the room where the team stayed, in bunk beds. To the left was the coach's room, which had three beds in it. The Dragons shared a bathroom with another team from DC. This is where being a girl in a sport of almost all boys gets complicated.

"Mo'ne couldn't stay in the dorms with the boys, so one of us had to stay up there in a hotel with her," my mom says.

Squirt, who works in construction, had hurt his back and couldn't work, so he was out on disability. He went to Bristol with me. My mom, she had to work and go to her college classes, so every few days she was traveling back and forth with Qu'ran, Maurice, and Mahogany, and some of my cousins. Her job was really nice to her so she could see me play. And she was packing up our house because our family was going to move to the suburbs. She made it to all the games when I pitched. I could hear her yelling, "Go, Mo!" from the stands.

On the first day of the tournament, the Dragons got a day of rest, while some of the other teams were playing.

"There wasn't anything to do in Bristol but eat, so on the first day, I watched all the games. And I'm like, 'Y'all can beat all of these teams,'" Squirt says. "The parents of the Taney kids looked at me like, 'Whatever, I have to go back to work on Monday.' I think they thought just getting to the regionals was a big accomplishment for the kids. But they hadn't seen the Monarch kids play before, so they thought the tournament was going to be so much harder than it was."

On Saturday, August 2, we played West Salisbury, Maryland. We beat them 11–1. Jared pitched and hit a two-run home run. The umpires called the game after four innings because of the mercy rule—after we got up on them by ten runs.

After the Maryland game, we played Newark National, from Delaware. They pitched Jack Hardcastle, this big kid who is their ace.

That game, I pitched and I played first base. While I was pitching, I was kind of in the zone. I didn't really realize it at the time, but I got ten strikeouts. I had seen a lot of people swing and miss, so striking kids out, it didn't really shock me. But I had never gotten that many strikeouts before. We beat Newark National 8–4.

After that, a lot more people started to remember my name.

"That's when reporters started calling me," Mom says. "I don't know how these people got my phone number. I told them, 'I'm not there, I'm in Philly.'"

"After that first weekend, a lot of the parents were like, 'Okay, we're stuck here,'" says Squirt.

Next up: Colonie, New York. That was a Friday, and it was a pretty crazy game. I played first and third base. We started out winning, but then we started losing. I think it's because we were in the opposite dugout from what we are usually in. We're usually in the home dugout one game and then the away dugout the next time. This game that didn't happen—we were in the away dugout two times in a row. There are a lot of superstitions in baseball, and for us, during the regionals, that was one of them.

We lost the game against New York, 5–3, but the game got a lot of attention. The word was spreading like wildfire that the Taney Dragons had a girl on their team and she was striking boys out.

The next game, we beat Northwest Washington, DC, 7–1.

After that, we went into the tournament bracket, and played New York again. The pressure was on because if we lost again, we would have to go home.

That game was pretty crazy, because we were down by three, and then we caught up. Then the next inning, we went ahead by three runs. Then in the last inning, they hit a home run to put them down by one run. I pitched at the very end of that game. Their number-three hitter was up, and we grounded him out. We won it 6–5.

Since it was so hot that day, after our game was over, I watched the other semifinal game, between Delaware and Toms River, in the rec room of the complex with Zion and Erik. We thought that we were gonna have to play Toms River, New Jersey. It seems like Toms River's always in the finals.

Toms River has a girl, and she's fast and can really hit.

"Everyone wanted to see that game, with her and Mo'ne on the field," my mom says.

I knew that if we played Toms River, I would have to be throwing well, because they can field and hit and pitch. We would have to go out there and bring our A-game. But Toms River would have to make it past Delaware.

Delaware had played them earlier in the tournament. It was a good game, even though Delaware lost. But after they lost, I think they realized they could beat them.

At one point in their rematch, Delaware got down 4–0. They brought in their ace, but Toms River was getting hits off of him, too. So it was pretty nerve-racking.

Near the end of the game, I got very superstitious. It seemed like every time I was lying on the floor, Delaware would get an out or score a run, and when I sat up, Toms River would score.

"Just lie down," Zion and Erik kept telling me. They wanted us to play against Delaware, since we had been hanging out with them a lot.

So I stayed lying down nearly the whole last inning, which was when Toms River brought in their hardest pitcher. Delaware started hitting off him and scored three runs, and they pulled through, and won 4–3.

Now we were gonna play Delaware in the championship, which was pretty exciting for us. The Delaware kids were the defending champs. Five of the kids on their team had gone on to Williamsport the year before. But they didn't get a lot of hits off of us the first time we played. Coach thought we would be okay as long as we were getting our bats on the ball.

Hitting was starting to be a problem, though. We had gone into a little slump.

The next day, we got a day off, so we practiced like we normally would. When we were hanging out together later on, some of the Delaware kids told us that in their practice, they had been preparing to hit against me.

On Sunday, August 10, at 6:00 p.m., we played against Delaware for the regional championship. The game was going to be nationally televised on ESPN. There were a lot of people in the stands and on the hill behind the stadium, supporting us. They believed we could make it to the Little League World Series.

Coach Alex wanted me to pitch. The pressure was on—a win would take us to the World Series, and help Jack and Jared fulfill their dream, which had now become the dream of everyone on the team.

Before the game, one of our coaches told us, "You gotta come out and score runs, and pile them on, and don't let them get anything."

We had to score more than two runs in the first inning, or we'd be off to a bad start. If we start out fast, we're pretty good, although sometimes we kind of get too upbeat, because we think we're gonna win.

I was a little bit nervous when the game started. I'm sure I wasn't the only one.

The first batter came to the plate. I threw one pitch and he grounded to the shortstop. One out. I got out in front of the second batter, then walked him. Then I struck the third batter out with a curveball. The cleanup hitter hit a grounder to third, forcing the runner out at second. Whew! Made it out of that inning.

"I was at home watching on ESPN," says Destiny. "I was like 'Go, Mo! Go, Mo!'"

Our at bat started out great, when Scott laid down a perfect bunt.

I flew out to center, but when Jahli singled through the middle, Scott was able to advance to third base. Jared ripped the first pitch he got all the way to the wall. Scott and Jahli scored, and Jared made it to second with a double.

Next up, Zion. Zion hit a grounder to third. But Zion's really fast. He beat out the throw. Jared scored.

All told, we scored four runs in the first inning, which we needed. Then we scored two in the next inning, and in the fifth inning, we scored two more. We were hitting well that game.

"And it was like no one could stop Mo'ne," says Zion. "Her curveball was working."

"A lot of people who I know from Philly were blowing up my phone—'I see you on TV, your little sister is pitching,'" says Qu'ran.

I had six strikeouts.

We ended up winning 8–0.

After we won, a lot of reporters wanted to interview us.

"I didn't know she was famous until she won that game," says Qayyah. "When she threw that last strike, it was crazy. A lot of reporters were interviewing us. I was tearing up, that's how excited I was."

A couple of reporters told me to challenge Clayton Kershaw to a "pitch-off"—whatever that is. Everyone was congratulating us, and people started asking me for my autograph and telling me they would remember my name and look for me in pro baseball.

"I was sitting on my couch and the news came on. There was a huge picture of her on the screen and she was the first story," says Abby. "That's how I found out she was going to the Little League World Series."

At that point, we had been in Bristol for ten straight days.

But after the championship, we took the bus straight to Williamsport, home of the Little League Baseball World Series.

CHAPTER 13
LIVING THE DREAM

ON MONDAY MORNING, AUGUST 11, 2014, THE TANEY DRAGONS boarded a bus to Williamsport for the Little League World Series. Little League was invented in Williamsport, in 1939. Every summer, two million kids play in eighty countries all around the world. And every summer, about seven thousand teams compete to try to get to the Little League World Series. Only sixteen elite US teams make it. The Taney Dragons were now one of those teams. We were the last team to get there, but now we were all experiencing our wildest dream, and we had gotten there together.

I had heard through the grapevine that I wouldn't be the only girl at the Little League World Series. When our bus first pulled up, the other girl, Emma March, was waiting at the gate.

"Hi, I'm Emma," she said, and she extended her hand. It turns out Emma was from Canada, and, since we were the only girls, we would be living in the same house. Over the week, we got to know each other. That was kind of cool.

Since the other teams had had to fly in from all over the country, they had gotten there earlier than we did, and they had been watching our game. Everyone was telling us, "Good job! Good job!"

We dropped off our stuff, then went straight to get our ID tags made. You need credentials to get into the complex, which they call the Grove and is kind of like an Olympic Village. No parents or friends or fans are allowed inside. You have to swipe a card and walk through a metal detector to get in and out. We were told not to check any social media or post pictures on Instagram, because our location would come up. If we wanted to take a picture, we could. But they told us not to post it until after we left. The security was very tight.

Right after we got our IDs, we went to get our uniforms. Since we were now representing the Mid-Atlantic Region, they replaced our navy-and-white Taney uniforms with medium-blue jerseys with burgundy on the shoulders that said *Mid-Atlantic Region* across the chest in burgundy script. We wore those with long white pants, and burgundy baseball caps with a medium-blue rim. The uniforms were nice, and blue is my favorite color. But the number on my shirt was no longer eleven. Now I was number three.

After that, we got our baseball bags, cleats, helmets, and batting gloves.

We thought that after we were done, there would still be some time to do our summer reading for school. But by the time we finished, it was dark, and everyone was excited, so no one could be quiet. Nobody read anything. Jahli played Nico and Vinz's song "Am I Wrong?" He played it a little too much in Williamsport.

The next morning, we met with the bat company Easton, to try out new bats, and we got our Oakley sunglasses. After that, we did the ESPN interview that they use to introduce you before each game.

"My name is Mo'ne Davis, and my favorite player is Chase Utley."

When they tape you, you never know if they're going to do something funny, like drop a fake spider on you while you're talking. They tried to drop the spider on me. I saw it when it was falling, so it didn't really scare me. But they got Zion good. We heard him screaming.

During the series, they showed all the kids who had a reaction to it. One kid from Chicago, he fell off the stool.

Dinner was served every day at four o'clock, which was really early, so sometimes we got hungry later. We didn't always want to go down to the night games to eat, because the lines were super long. So at night, the coaches would order us pizza and buffalo wings.

Our parents stayed in Williamsport, in hotels. The tournament lasts two weeks. We could only see them after games in a tent outside the Grove. At first just Squirt was staying over. My mom would drive back and forth from Philly, and bring my brothers and sister, and my brother's friends—I call them my cousins, and one of them my brother—from South Philly. But then she would have to go back to work.

Qayyah and Yirah would also come up on different days.

"We saw men and kids on other teams wearing Mo'ne T-shirts and a lot of posters and signs," says Qayyah.

"I had a shirt, too," says Yirah. "Mine had a picture of us three."

During the week, Emma and I got to know each other, and I got to see her play a little bit. She was really nice, and she told me a lot about her team. Emma is also a pitcher and she plays first base. She played on the same team as her brother, who catches sometimes.

....

Play started in the double-elimination bracket on Thursday, August 14, but we didn't have to play till the next day. Since the complex had this great rec room with a TV, Ping-Pong, video games, and lots of other stuff, me, Scott, Zion, Jared, and Jahli went there to hang out. I was playing Ping-Pong against Zion. One time, I hit the ball off the table and it rolled over by the TV. Zion went over to get it, and while he was getting the ball, he looked up at the screen.

"Oh, hey, *Sport Science* is coming up," he said. *Sport Science* is this show on ESPN about the science and engineering of athletics. "Wait, it's your name!" he shouted.

"What?" I asked him.

"I said it's your name," he said. "Like, you're gonna be on *Sport Science!*"

I didn't understand what he was talking about, but then the show came on, and it *was* about me—that was surprising and kind of weird!

They said that my pitching relied on "pristine mechanics," not my size or my strength. They said that every time I throw the ball, the place where I let go of it—the release point—never changes by more than three degrees. That's pretty precise! They said my arm moves 15 percent slower than a major league pitcher's, but they still clocked my fastball at seventy miles per hour. Since we play on a smaller field, they said that batters have to react as fast to my pitches as a major leaguer would to a pitcher throwing a ninety-one-mile-per-hour fast-ball. They also compared my body mechanics to Phillies closer Jonathan Papelbon. He's from Philly, and we're from Philly, so that was cool. It was pretty nice to be a thirteen-year-old being compared to thirty-five-year-olds!

A little while after that, Eli and Jared came up to me and said, "You gotta come out of the Grove and go to the field, people are looking for you."

They said it was these kids from North Philly who knew me. At first I was a little confused, but then I was like, "Okay, maybe I *do* know them."

We thought they meant, like, four people, but when we got down to the field, it was a whole lot of people, and I didn't know any of them. They wanted our pictures and autographs. On one hand that was kind of cool, but it was also kind of awkward. And there were a lot of adults—that was kind of creepy. We signed a few autographs, then Eli and Jared left us, and Scott, Zion, and I kind of got stuck in a corner. After a while, we just started walking away, then turned a corner and ran as fast as we could back to the Grove.

Later, we bumped into the Great Lakes and New England teams. They were having fun, having a battle with really bad funny raps, and combining their names and calling themselves "New Lakes." We were just laughing at them. That's when we first started talking to the kids from the Great Lakes team, Jackie Robinson West, from Chicago. They were the only other city team. Just knowing that another team had been inspired by Jackie Robinson, just like the Monarchs were, made me think a lot about the sacrifices he made so we could be here.

Before our championship series began, we started getting more superstitious. We reminded each other to be careful not to step on any lines on the baseball field before the game. I was careful to put some change or my barnstorming wristband in my back pocket. Jared made sure to sleep with a ball beneath his pillow. Scott had his orange ball. Every time he had it with him in the dugout we would win, so he brought it. And Zion kept praying before our games.

Game 1: Mid-Atlantic vs. Southeast Region: South Nashville, Tennessee
When I put on my uniform, on Friday, August 15, I put seven one-dollar bills in one of my pants pockets and a nickel in the other one for good luck.

Our opening-round game started at three that afternoon.

It was the first time we had walked out onto the field of Howard J. Lamade Stadium, one of the two stadiums the Little League World Series is played on. The stadiums have this really nice grass called Kentucky bluegrass. The clay on the mound and base paths is almost orange and really smooth—a lot different from what we normally play on. I was careful not to step on the lines.

The stands at Lamade run along the first- and third-base lines. When we were warming up, they were already pretty crowded. There is also this big hill behind the out-field fence. That hill was packed with people sitting in lawn chairs. There was a sidewalk behind that part of the hill, and the hill kept going on the other side of that. That hill got packed, too. Eventually, about thirty-five thousand people watched us.

Coach Alex decided I would be pitching that day. In between warm-up pitches, I could see our families sitting in the front row along the third-base line, in the VIP seats for parents. For the first time, I could see my mom, but I couldn't hear her.

ESPN2 was televising the game, and there were cameras all over the place.

Reporters were walking around with signs, asking, "Who are Jared's parents?" "Who are Mo'ne's parents?" The parents raised their hands, or other parents pointed them out, so that the cameras could find them during the game.

I can't remember who, but right before we started, someone said, "That's why we made it here, so try to savor every moment that you can."

The whole situation was super, super exciting.

I breathed deeply and thought about Jackie Robinson, and how his courage generations ago helped me make it here.

But I was nervous.

I was biting my nails, until Jared came up and hit a three-run home run.

Later on, he told a reporter, "I just wanted to help Mo'ne out. Because I knew she was going to do well, but she needs a couple of runs. As soon as it went out, I was very excited."

Jared, he's nice, he's very intelligent, and he's very funny. Although he acts like he's the oldest, Jared is the youngest member of our team, so it was amazing that he could do that.

After Jared homered, the nerves kind of went away, and we were just all telling each other, "Just go out there and have fun."

I was able to get the first six batters out.

One of the things I remember most was that it was

really loud in the stadium.

"We were wasting our vocal cords screaming at each other," Jahli remembers. "So we started using hand signals."

On one of my at bats, I got a pitch down the middle. I swung hard but got under it, and popped it up. If I had hit it straight away, I probably would have hit it out. I think their pitcher knew it. When I was running back from first base to the dugout near third, he gave me a high five, and he was like, "Good job," like he wanted to say, "Thank you."

We could hear the crowd getting louder, but I wasn't really thinking about why. I wouldn't find out till later that a lot of them were there to cheer for us because I was a girl on the mound, and I was striking out boys. A lot of people were cheering for *me*!

In the last inning, while I was pitching, the count was 3–2, with two outs. All of a sudden, the stadium got really loud.

"We got everybody to stand up and start cheering and clapping," my mom says.

"The whole stadium started to say, 'Go, Mo'ne!'" says Yirah. "I thought I was dreaming for a minute because I didn't think this would ever really happen to one of us."

The noise got to the batter, and he stepped out of the batter's box.

The umpire told us, "Let's just wait until this kind of calms down."

"This whole line of reporters started lining up on their knees, on the ground, right in front of us," Squirt says.

I stood on the mound and kind of blocked things out, so I didn't get distracted.

"I don't know where she gets that from," my mom says. "She's always calm. I could holler all night long, and Mo'ne will be so calm. Sometimes I'm like, 'Did you even take in anything I said?' And she'll still be calm."

"Mo'ne, she's a breed unto herself," says Qu'ran. "She's cut from a different cloth."

"I was just wowed, watching her," says Coach Brady, who came up to watch the game.

When the batter stepped back in the box, I got set, went into my windup, and threw a fastball right down the middle.

I struck the kid out.

We won: 4–0.

That made me the first girl to pitch a shutout in Little League history. I threw eight strikeouts and only gave up two hits.

"Everybody was calling me," says Qu'ran. "It was crazy!"

The Little League officials took my jersey and told

me that they were going to put it in the National Baseball Hall of Fame. They gave me a replacement.

They had a bunch of us do a press conference. By now, I was used to getting interviewed. You just gotta be pretty calm. Sometimes you get the same question over and over, but sometimes you get really cool questions.

I have this problem with one-word answers, like "Yes" and "No," and short ones, like "I don't know" or "I'm not sure." So I try to keep my answers at a middle length, because three-word answers can be super dull. And I try not to be too hyped, because if you're too hyped, you could look kind of goofy.

"There were all these different people, and she was sitting there making jokes," Squirt says. "She had an answer for everything they said. I was like, 'How does she do this?' Nobody helped her, and she had no time to practice."

But I didn't really feel comfortable about how many of the questions were directed at me. We are a team, and you can't win a game by yourself. It's not like I can pitch to myself and then go catch it. Everybody on the team was part of our win. Sometimes I thought my teammates could give better answers, so I passed the question to them.

CHAPTER 14
WE'RE OUT

AFTER OUR FIRST GAME, WE HAD BATTING PRACTICE AND fielding practice, and Coach Alex changed the batting order. Up until that point, it had started with Scott, me, Jahli, Jared, and Zion. But he wanted to get our strongest hitters—Jahli, Jared, and Zion—up more often to give them a lot of at bats. He dropped me to sixth.

Batting sixth is fine with me. When you're at the top of the lineup, you're most likely a good hitter, so the pitcher will throw you a lot more curveballs to keep you off balance. When you're sixth, you get a lot more fastballs, which are easier to hit.

When I was pitching, Coach Alex was paying attention to how many balls I threw. Kids in my age group can't throw more than eighty-five pitches a day, and depending on how many pitches you throw, you're required to rest a certain number of days. I had thrown sixty-five pitches against Tennessee, so I was eligible to pitch again in game three.

Game 2: Sunday, August 17: Mid-Atlantic vs. Southwest Region: Pearland, Texas

After our first game people were very hyped. The Taney Dragons were the talk of the tournament and a lot of people were rooting for us to win.

Jared was up next to pitch. I played third base.

I got my first hit that game, and I got an RBI. But the game was pretty crazy. When Jack was running home to score, the catcher tagged him super hard, and he got hit in the mouth. His tooth cut his lip, and his lip was swollen and bleeding. He had to leave the game.

After Jack left, Coach moved me to shortstop.

The game was really back and forth. It was like they would score, then we would score. At one point, Jared gave up a two-strike home run and got really upset. We had to try to calm him down.

But in the last inning, we came back.

Scott came up to bat.

"It's my job to get on base," he says.

Since a lot of teams know how fast he is and that he can beat out a bunt, Texas pulled their third baseman in really close to home plate.

"The third baseman was right on top of me, since I always bunt down the third-base line," says Scott. "So I dragged a bunt down the first-base line. It was my first drag-bunt hit ever!"

Jahli was up next. He struck out, and then Jared flew out. But then Zion hit a triple.

"When Scott was rounding second, I was saying to myself, 'Coach Alex, send him, send him home,'" says Zion.

He did and Scott scored, which tied the game. Then Tai was up. There were two outs, and he was down 0–2 in the count, and Zion was on third. Tai hit a ground ball to the shortstop, which should have ended the inning. But the shortstop rushed and overthrew to first. Tai was safe at first, and Zion scored.

We won: 7–6.

After the game, someone told me that I was only the sixth girl to get a hit in Little League World Series history.

In the press conference afterward, Tai said that his walk-off single was probably one of the best things that had ever happened to him in his baseball career.

"A win's a win," Coach Alex said. "We just felt good."

Later on, I learned that we had a larger television audience than the Yankees–Red Sox game on *Sunday Night Baseball*. ESPN2 never outdraws ESPN.

But by then, we were definitely in a batting slump.

While we were focused on our next game, everyone was talking about the Taney Dragons. Our pins were the hottest pins to trade at the tournament—everywhere we went, people wanted them.

All of a sudden, I had turned into a role model for girls. The fact that I was playing with the boys and striking them out showed people that girls can play against boys in sports and be as good as they are, if not better. And that you can't just expect us to be real emotional—girls can have nerves of steel.

I didn't mind that. It was kind of nice.

"There was a lot of buzz about her. People were starting to ask for her autograph," Miss Robin says. "The kids were all signing balls. Someone told me one of her signed balls was going for two hundred dollars on eBay."

"At the World Series, I would see big, husky guys with Mo'ne Davis shirts on," says Coach Brady. "Seeing them wearing her name on their shirts and on their backs was just so thrilling for me."

"I heard a boy say that his hero was Mo'ne, and that

he wanted to pitch like her," Dr. Sands, the head of my school and Scott and Jahli's school, remembers.

We didn't know it at the time, but while we were playing, our friends and classmates and families back home were cheering us on.

"We were watching Mo'ne on TV," says Qayyah.

"Some of the kids in my school were saying, 'You seen that girl on ESPN playing baseball? She's striking everyone out!'" says Qu'ran. "I would just sit around and say, 'Yeah, she's good. I think she's gonna make it to the major leagues.'"

Qu'ran was the first person to tell me that I was blowing up on Twitter.

"I kept seeing these Kevin Durant tweets like, 'This youngster's out here throwing flames—and she is a girl. I love it. Hashtag 'It's a new day,'" says Qu'ran. "But she ain't retweet, so I thought she must not know what's going on."

But when he told me what was happening, I had seen it already.

People like Michelle Obama, Magic Johnson, Russell Wilson, and Mike Trout tweeted me. It was super, super surprising.

All across Philly, there was Taney-mania. People were watching us on TV at home, at the neighborhood bar, in the TV section of electronics stores—even Philadelphia's mayor, Michael Nutter, held a watch party on the plaza outside of City Hall.

My friends at Springside were celebrating, too.

"We had a sign made running down the fence along the side of our playing fields, and it had a little Taney cap, and it said, 'We heart Mo'ne, We heart Jahli, We heart Scott'—the kids who were students here," says Dr. Sands. "Then we had watch parties, where we put these big screens on the field and hundreds of people came, and tons of news trucks were up and down the street. We sold ballpark food—popcorn and Philadelphia Water Ice. People had blankets and lawn chairs and sat out on the lawn. It was an old-fashioned feel-good moment."

Later on, someone told me that during the game, the boys' soccer team started shouting "Mo'ne, Mo'ne, Mo'ne" over and over. The kids at our school are really great.

August 19, 2014

It was day five of the Little League World Series and the Ping-Pong battle in the rec room was on. I had just lost, and was just sitting there on my phone. I got this text from Squirt. It was a picture of me on the cover of *Sports Illustrated* magazine.

At first I was a little confused. I knew that I had talked to them, but no one knew that they were planning to put me on the cover. Yet someone had sent a picture to

Squirt, and Squirt sent the picture to me.

Later on, this guy from Williamsport we called Cousin Josh bought copies for everyone on the team. When I signed one for him, it was the first time I saw it in person.

I didn't know that the cover of *Sports Illustrated* was that big of a deal. I didn't read the article for a while. But people started telling me that I had bumped Kobe Bryant off the cover. Then some of the kids on other teams started saying that if you got on the cover of *Sports Illustrated*, it was a curse. There's a long list of people who had had bad luck after being on the cover. Like the LA Dodgers. When Matt Kemp and Magic Johnson appeared on the cover in May 2012, they had the best record in baseball. But out of their next eleven games, they lost eight of them. And the Denver Broncos quarterback Peyton Manning. In February 2014, he was featured on the cover for setting all sorts of passing and touchdown records. But right after that, the Broncos lost one of the most lopsided Super Bowl games in NFL history, 43–8.

It was right around that time Scott lost his orange ball.

Game 3: Wednesday, August 20, 7:30 p.m.: Mid-Atlantic vs. Western Region: Las Vegas, Nevada
We had reached the finals of the winner's bracket. The

winner of the game would go on to the championship and the loser would play in the semifinals.

People lined up early in the morning to get tickets for our game against Las Vegas. It rained lightly during the day, but then the sun came out. It was a little humid but there was a nice breeze.

I was gonna be the starting pitcher, but they would pull me out after thirty-five pitches so they could save me for the finals in case we made it that far. Erik would pitch after I came out. If we won this game, we would move on to the US finals. If we lost, we would play an elimination game against Chicago. The winner of that game would meet the winner of our game in the finals.

We watched Nevada's last game online on ESPN on Coach Alex's computer. In my last two starts, I'd thrown fourteen strikeouts and hadn't allowed any runs in the twelve innings I'd pitched. But Vegas would be my toughest test of the season since they were a team that was used to blowing people out. In their last eight games, they had scored seventy-nine runs and had given up just two runs per game to their opponents. The team's top three hitters—Austin Kryszczuk, Brennan Holligan, and Brad Stone—were very tough, and Austin was probably the best hitter in the whole tournament.

Our game plan included not pitching Austin anything in the middle of the plate or away—or he could make me pay for it. But we felt pretty confident since all season long I'd given up no more than two hits per inning. We talked about the idea of sometimes intentionally walking their batters. And we wanted to make them earn anything they got. No matter what happened we were not gonna show any bad body language.

There were a little more than thirty-four thousand people on hand in the stadium—more people than live in all of Williamsport, and about nine thousand more people than were at the Phillies game that day. Vegas wanted to be the away team so they could hit first and get on the board quickly.

In the first inning I was a little nervous and my pitches kept sailing kind of high.

Their first batter got a leadoff single.

Austin was batting second. I threw him a curve. As soon as the ball left my hand, I knew that I'd made a mistake. It didn't break hard enough—it just didn't move. Austin ripped it to right center field and the ball went all the way to the wall. He got a triple and the leadoff batter scored.

In the bottom of the first, we had two runners on base and two outs. Then Jack ripped a fly ball to right field and their fielder had to dive and make a catch. *Unbelievable!*

A third strike was called on Jahli. *What!* It seemed

like the strike zone was moving around an awful lot.

Top of the second, I got one kid out then gave up a two-run home run. They were up 3–0, and my pitch count was kind of high—fifty-five—so Coach Alex brought Erik in after two and one-third innings. I had walked one, given up six hits and three runs, and struck out six batters, including Austin, Brennan, and Brad. I didn't even think that Austin could strike out. But then I struck him out. It was one of the first games in the World Series that he didn't hit a home run. So I was really happy after that.

We got the bases loaded and two runners on in the fourth, and two runners on base in the fifth, but we couldn't get them in to score. Austin was on the mound that day. On top of being a great hitter, he is a pretty good pitcher. He was sharp that day.

Erik kept them really close—we were down just 3–1 going into the sixth inning. But the wheels came off in the sixth inning.

Toward the end of the game, our pitchers weren't throwing strikes, and we walked people. Their kids started hitting us. One kid got an RBI double, Austin got an RBI single, Brandon hit a two-run homer, and we had a passed ball—when the ball gets past the catcher and the runners advance. They got five runs in the top of the last inning. We didn't score in the bottom of the sixth.

But when I came up to bat, a lot of people cheered, which was nice.

They won: 8–1.

Because I gave up Vegas's winning run, I was charged with the loss. I didn't get any hits either. Vegas definitely became the team to beat. For a super quick second, I wondered if the *Sports Illustrated* cover had cursed our team or maybe just Scott's lost ball.

Later we found out that almost five million people watched our game on ESPN, which made it the highest-rated Little League game ever.

Game 4: Thursday, August 21: Mid-Atlantic vs. Great Lakes Region: Chicago Jackie Robinson West
On the morning of our game against Chicago, Philadelphia Phillie Ryan Howard came to the rec room and played Ping-Pong and video games with us.

There was a super, super amount of hype going into this all-elimination game—whoever lost would be out. Plus, a lot of people thought it was a big deal that the two city teams were meeting up. And maybe it was, since we were proving that kids who live in the city like baseball and, when we have good programs to play in, we can be great.

The Taney Dragons threw Erik that day, which was really smart, because when Texas played Chicago, their lefty pitcher did pretty well against the Chicago batting lineup. Eric is a lefty and throws a mean curve that can dive into the dirt.

"But before the game started, there was a rain delay," says Zion. "Mo'ne, Eli, and Tai went to sleep in the dugout."

In the first inning, Zion hit a double off the centerfield wall. Then Jared got on base. Then Jack got a single, and drove Zion and Jared in. So we started out up 2-0, which is an okay start for us, but not great.

Then Great Lakes came back and scored four runs in the bottom of the first inning.

In the second inning, Coach Alex pulled Erik out of the game but Great Lakes scored two more runs anyhow. We didn't get on the board again until the fourth inning, when Zion hit a two-run single. That made it 6-4.

We got another run in the fifth, when Kai hit a homer.

Except for Zion, who was a perfect two for two, our bats were pretty silent. I didn't get any hits.

We gave up three unearned runs by errors.

We lost: 6-5.

That was it for us in the tournament.

"Some people think, 'Aww, they didn't win.' But it was amazing just to get there," says Coach Steve. "We had just one bad game."

That night, we tried to go out to eat, but TGI Fridays,

Olive Garden, and Denny's were all packed. Only fast-food restaurants were left, so we decided to go to Taco Bell.

"You guys are from the Little League World Series, right?" the guy behind the counter said to us.

"Yeah . . ."

"Good luck," he told us. "I hope you win it all."

"We're out, sir," we told him. "We just lost."

But even though I was disappointed, I thought about how my mom started out working at Taco Bell when she was a teenager and struggling to make it in life, and here I was back at Taco Bell on one of the most exciting days of my life.

After we ate, we went back to the dorm area.

Scott, Jahli, Zion, and I went to the rec room. We started throwing squishy balls with Drew from the West team. All of a sudden, there were, like, fifty balls, and we all started throwing them at each other. Then people started turning out the lights. The TV was off, but all the video games were lighting up, so it looked pretty cool. Then Pierce and Ed from the Chicago team walked in, and Ed got hit in the head by a ball.

After that, Zion and I went over to the Chicago team's dorm. There were a lot of kids there—Chicago kids, the Australian kids, some West kids. Everyone was playing catch with another squishy ball. Even though we had lost a big game, it was so much fun hanging out with kids from all these other teams.

Sunday, August 24: Little League World Series US Championship: West vs. Great Lakes

On Sunday night, in the finals—after the Asia-Pacific team beat the team from Japan in the international finals—Jackie Robinson West beat Nevada and won the Little League US World Series Championship. We were really excited for our friends. It was a big win for them. Vegas has the best hitters in the country. Earlier in the week, Nevada had even beaten Chicago, 10–1. We were disappointed for the Vegas kids, since they were also our friends. But they got to come in second, which is a very big deal.

That's just how baseball goes.

So at the end of the Series, the Jackie Robinson kids had a 5–2 record, Vegas was 3–2, and Pearland and Mid-Atlantic both were at 2–2, but we had beaten Pearland in our head-to-head matchup.

We came in third out of seven thousand teams.

We felt pretty good about that.

The next day South Korea beat Chicago to win the entire World Series.

CHAPTER 15
MO-MENTUM

WE LEFT WILLIAMSPORT EARLY THE NEXT MORNING, MONDAY, August 25. We were exhausted, and my teammates were asleep, or talking on the phones with their moms and dads, telling them where we were so their parents could meet the bus when it got back to Philly.

When we reached the city limits, a bunch of police motorcycles and cars started escorting us. Then the bus pulled up to LOVE Park, at the end of Benjamin Franklin Parkway, which runs between the Philadelphia Museum of Art and City Hall, where there's this great red sculpture, *LOVE*.

When we stopped, the mayor came onto the bus with

a Taney hat and T-shirt on and congratulated us, and told us that they were holding a celebration for us. The plaza was pretty packed with people of all ages and races.

When we got off the bus, the police made way for us through the crowd. Everyone was cheering—I even saw two sophomores from my school. That was our first experience back home with "Taney-mania."

After the ceremony was over, I took my braids out, dropped my stuff off at home, and went to get my hair pressed—we were taking another bus to New York later on because we had been invited to be on the *Today* show!

Around dinnertime, we rode the bus to New York with our families. We pulled into Times Square at about nine o'clock that night, which was pretty cool, because we got to see all the lights. If you haven't seen the lights in Times Square before, go on the internet so you can see them. Then we checked into our hotel and went to dinner. For dessert, I had a brownie smoothie with fudge and vanilla—it was delicious!

When we went back to the hotel, everybody's parents were telling us to go to bed, because we had to get up at four a.m. and it would still be dark outside. So I unpacked my stuff and took my shower. But when people tell me that I have to fall asleep early, I try to make myself go to sleep, but I just can't. So I watched the VMAs—Beyoncé's performance was on. Eventually, I fell asleep.

At the *Today* show, we stood outside waving to the cameras for a while. A lot of people knew who we were, and they were cheering for our team.

Then we got to meet Matt Lauer and Savannah Guthrie. Tamron Hall took a selfie with me and I acted silly and stuck out my tongue. But everything happened so fast, I don't remember what they asked us.

After we left the *Today* show, we went straight to *Good Morning America*. Then we went to the NBA Store to look at jerseys and things. When we came back home to Philly, I just went to sleep.

When we went back to Marian Anderson, our friends and other people were congratulating us. Also, a lot of people I didn't know were saying, "Congratulations, good job!"

People started telling me that I was an inspiration to girls.

"I saw these two boys playing catch, and one of them said, 'I want to be Mo'ne,'" says Squirt. "Then the other one said, 'No, I want to be Mo'ne!'"

That Wednesday, the city held a big parade for us. We rode through downtown on a float. A lot of people came out of their jobs to cheer for us and take pictures, and we saw a lot of people that we knew.

"There were, like, a lot of people there, and I saw her

on the float," says Nahla. "And when she came off the float, her mom let me come in the gate, and I said hi to her. But the mayor was like, 'No, no, back away from the gate. No autographs.' And I'm like, 'I know her, she's my best friend!'"

All of my teammates were on the float. Erik was jumping around, doing his dance—playing the air bongos.

We drove around City Hall, then went all the way down Broad Street to FDR Park, down by the stadium, just like the Philadelphia Phillies had when they won the World Series when I was seven. Then the mayor promised to renovate five new baseball fields. We'd shown the world that city kids really do love to play baseball, and that we can be really good. A lot of parents were telling the mayor that they wanted their kids to play.

After that, all of the Taney Dragons were invited to a Phillies game to throw out the first pitch against the Washington Nationals. At first, I was kind of nervous, but after a little while that went away. All twelve Taney Dragons stood near the mound in a line, and twelve Phillies lined up at home plate, and the Dragons all threw our balls at the same time.

I threw the ball to Jonathan Papelbon, the player *Sport Science* said I am a lot like. He signed a baseball and gave it to me, and told me that I had a lot of talent and to use it. I also got to meet Chase Utley for the first time, which was a big deal since he is my favorite player.

We got Phillies jerseys and our pictures taken with the players.

"She was sending us all these pictures," says Nahla. "'I'm with Chase Utley. OMG, OMG, OMG!'"

"That was her lifelong dream," says Abby.

Around Labor Day, I got to go to the WNBA playoffs in Minnesota. I got to sit on the Minnesota bench and I met Lindsay Whalen, Simone Edwards, and Maya Moore. I met Brittney Griner in the Phoenix locker room. That was super exciting. I was surprised to know that so many people knew who I was, and Brittney Griner was really nice to me. A lot of reporters were interested in me. The assistant coach from Minnesota said, "I haven't seen this many cameras since we won the championship. Get out of her face and let her talk to us!"

It was pretty cool to get to talk to everybody, and somebody took a selfie with me. When I was watching the game, I realized that a lot of point guards don't use their left hand. So I decided that I should keep using my left hand just to get better.

The next morning, I flew to Los Angeles to be on *The Queen Latifah Show*. Queen Latifah was one of the first successful female rappers, and she was a power forward on her high school basketball team. She is very nice, and I could tell that she was from the East Coast.

From there, a car took us to Dodger Stadium, where I was going to meet Clayton Kershaw and throw out the first pitch at the Dodgers' game against the Washington Nationals.

I really like Los Angeles—it's a really modern city, and a lot different from Philly, which is very old. But it took us forever to get to the stadium because the highway was packed—they say the highways are always packed there. We got off and took some side streets, but they were packed, too. When we got there, they gave me a blue-and-white Dodgers cap and a jersey to put on top of my pink-and-white-striped shirt. I also had on jeans and black-and-pink sneakers.

Then, I got to meet two of the Dodgers' superstars: Yasiel Puig, an All-Star outfielder, and Adrian Gonzalez, who is an All Star and winner of the Gold Glove award for the league's best fielder. Yasiel is from Cuba, and he asked me for my autograph. Then I got in a fake argument with Matt Kemp about who should get to throw out the first pitch for the game, Queen Latifah or me.

I threw out the first pitch from in front of the pitcher's mound, but I wasn't nervous at all.

During the game, I got to sit in Magic Johnson's

seat. He wasn't there, but I did get to talk on the phone with him, and that was pretty cool, since he's one of the Dodgers' owners.

That night we took a red-eye home. When we got off the plane, my mom drove me straight to school, since I had missed the first day. When the head of the middle school, Miss Sakovics, brought me out into the hall, everyone just came over to hug me.

A few moments later Nahla walked by with her head down.

"Hi, Nahla," I said.

"I thought it was just a random person," says Nahla. "Then I turned around to see who it was. I couldn't believe it was her because she had just texted me that she wasn't coming back till the next week. I put my hand over my mouth and was like, 'Oh my gosh!'"

Actually, she looked like she had just seen Jesus.

"I ran down the hallway yelling, 'Mo'ne's back! Mo'ne's back!'" she says.

I was happy to see my friends and go back to being regular Mo'ne. Even though they were congratulating me, at the same time my friends were treating me normal. Someone told me that Dr. Sands had held an assembly and told everyone just to act cool and let things be as normal as possible.

After school, I went to soccer practice in my street clothes, and the team took a soccer selfie with a caption that said, *Mo'ne joins the soccer team.*

That Friday, Scott and I went to a WNBA luncheon in New York. We took the train to the city, and got to sit at the same table as the commissioner and meet Skylar Diggins, Becky Hammon, and Swin Cash.

Afterward, we went to the MLB Fan Cave and got vials of dirt from Dodger Stadium, Yankee Stadium, Fenway Park, and the stadiums of the Giants, the Angels, the Twins, the Pirates, and the Nationals. I keep mine in my baseball bag.

While we were there, we met Jackie Robinson's daughter, Miss Sharon. And Spike Lee turned out to be there, so we met him, too.

A few days later, on September 8, Scott and I were on *The Tonight Show*. When we were sitting in the greenroom—the room that they put you in before they bring you onto the stage—I met the Roots, the hip-hop group from South Philly that is the house band for *The Tonight Show Starring Jimmy Fallon*.

One of the Roots kept calling everyone "nephew."

I was sitting on a sofa, and Jimmy Fallon walked in. But he walked right by me, straight over to Scott, and said, "Oh, Mo'ne, you cut your hair!"

Scott was startled.

It was so funny—you should have seen the look on Scott's face!

I was supposed to pitch a baseball to Jimmy inside a batting cage.

"But to protect the audience, they went to a Wiffle ball, which she had never thrown before—ever," says Scott. "We got a five-minute practice in the hallway, and she didn't throw anything that even came near the plate."

Right before we went onstage, this guy came up to me and told me he was a Wiffle ball champion. He told me that if I throw the ball with the holes up, it will go up. If I hold it with the holes down, it will go down. If they are left, it will go left. It worked.

When we got on the stage, Jimmy did a funny introduction of us. Then all of a sudden he said, "Now, the time on the show when we do random dancing." I didn't know what he was talking about—I wasn't really ready for it.

I'm not the best dancer.

I went along with it, and Scott did the dance that Erik on our team does—playing the air bongos.

Then Jimmy made a joke and said random dancing was my idea.

What?!

After that, he put on this crazy red helmet, and did a

pretend stare-down, and talked a lot of trash. I blew the ball past him a bunch of times. Scott and I were laughing the whole time.

"On the last pitch, I told her to hit him," says Scott.

Jimmy stormed the mound and gave me a hug.

"Mo'ne Davis from the Taney Dragons," he said to the audience. "Remember her name!"

After that, we got to meet Macklemore and sit onstage when he performed his song "Arrows." Macklemore's dancing is pretty wild.

Then one day, kind of out of the blue, my mother said, "You wanna do a commercial with Spike Lee?"

"Sure," I told her. "When?"

"In two weeks."

When she told me the date, I already had told my friend that I was gonna come to her party, and we had the day off from school. I figured we'd finish filming the commercial in time for me to go, since the party started at seven.

On that Friday, we filmed the scene of me walking up to the mound, and hitting in the batting cage, and stuff like that. But we ran really late and I missed my friend's party. Being kind of famous isn't always that fun.

Saturday was the most packed day of filming. At six thirty in the morning, we filmed me running up the

Philadelphia Museum of Art steps, like Sylvester Stallone did in a scene in the movie *Rocky*. If you don't know about it, you can find it on YouTube. Then we drove to my new house, and they filmed the entire family.

Then we came back to Philly, and went straight to South Street to Lazaro's, my favorite pizza place, with my brothers and sister. After the Little League World Series was over, Lazaro's put the Mo'ne cheesesteak on the menu, which has Cheez Whiz and fried onions in it. I think the way I eat my cheesesteaks—with mayo, melted American cheese, salt and pepper, and ketchup—must have been too boring.

That Sunday, Spike Lee filmed me at Marian Anderson, then interviewed me. After that, I went straight to our baseball game against the Full Armor Falcons, a team from Northeast Philly that plays in the Tri-State Elite League.

I kept thinking my life would return to how it normally was before the Little League World Series, but it didn't.

On September 25, my Taney and Monarch teammates and I traveled on our barnstorming tour bus up to Cooperstown, where we played an exhibition game and I donated my Little League jersey to the National Baseball Hall of Fame. A lot of our families came. Coach Brady came, and so did Miss Mamie Johnson. The mayor of Cooperstown read a proclamation that designated it Taney Dragons and Anderson Monarchs Day.

The Hall of Fame is really cool. It has all sorts of things from baseball history—from sandlot games to the Negro Leagues to Hank Aaron chasing Babe Ruth's home run record to baseball in the Caribbean.

"I haven't seen Mo'ne's jersey. Where is it?" Coach Brady asked my mom while we were walking through the museum.

"Are you kidding me?" my mom said. "They took that as soon as she finished the game that day!"

During the ceremony, Coach Steve made a nice speech about me.

"She pitched two complete-game shutouts, eighteen strikeouts, no walks. And she captured the hearts and the imaginations of girls not only in this country, but around the world. I can't think of a more perfect ending to an incredible summer and a more fitting place to end it than at the Hall at Cooperstown," he said. "We're just so proud that her jersey will be on display here, to be an inspiration to just countless generations of girls to come."

Then I handed my jersey back to the head of the Hall of Fame, for them to officially put in the museum.

It was kind of hard to hand it over because it was a special jersey, but I have another one. And to see my shutout jersey here with the other jerseys would be amazing.

"She is going to be the first lady to go to the major leagues," Miss Mamie Johnson told a reporter. "That's where I want her to be. If you want to do something, you can do it, because I did it, and did it well. And she can do it, too."

From October 8 to 10, ESPN held its Women + Sports Summit in California. I was invited to participate in a panel called "Voices of the Future."

A few days later the Women's Sports Foundation held its annual Salute to Women in Sports in New York. The Women's Sports Foundation was founded by tennis legend Billie Jean King to support girls and women in sports and physical activity. I met Muhammad Ali's daughter, Laila Ali. I hope you know who Muhammad Ali is—he's one of the greatest boxers of all time, and he's one of the most well-known people in the whole world. You can Google him. Laila Ali was a women's boxer, and used to be the world champion. She was really nice and spent time talking to me for a few minutes, until she had to go sit at a different table.

On October 24, I traveled to San Francisco to throw out the first pitch at game four of the MLB World Series, when the San Francisco Giants played the Kansas City Royals. The night before the game, I got to see my friends from Jackie Robinson West. The MLB was going to honor them, too, and they were going to stand with me when I threw out the first pitch. Pierce, DJ, and Trey and I were up until three o'clock in the morning, playing pool. But I woke up at five a.m. because the time zone is different, so it was kind of weird.

Before the game that day, we went to a clinic with a lot of kids and teenagers. Jimmy Rollins was there. J-Roll plays for the Phillies and is one of the best defensive shortstops in baseball. And I got to talk to Chase Utley on the phone—he was funny. He asked me if I was taller than Jimmy Rollins. Jimmy Rollins is a little short, but he's definitely taller than I am. I found out that San Francisco is chilly and foggy and rainy a lot, and it was drizzling when we drove to the stadium. I started feeling pretty nervous. But when we got there, my nerves started to calm down.

When you first get to AT&T Park, the first thing you see is a giant Coca-Cola bottle, then you see a huge glove next to it. It looks like the bottle is going to pour Coke in the glove. People say AT&T is a pitcher's park, since the outfield wall is so far away. It is right next to San Francisco Bay. During the game, people park boats and row kayaks in the bay, right on the other side of the stadium, because they hope they'll get the ball after a "splash hit," a home run hit into the bay.

We walked across a bridge to Pier 48, then came into the stadium from the ground level. When I saw the field, it seemed small, even though it's not.

When we went inside, I met the officials from the Giants and the MLB. Spike Lee was there, too, behind home plate.

On television, the commercial Spike Lee filmed of me ran during the game, and I made fun of the insult "throwing like a girl" by reminding people that girls can throw seventy miles per hour and play baseball with the boys.

Right before the game started, they took me behind home plate while they introduced the Chicago kids, played a video about them, and announced the names of some of them. When they ran out to the field and stood by the mound, I started wondering how I was going to do. It was wet out, I was cold, and I hadn't had a chance to warm my arm up. Then they played a video to introduce me and called my name. There was a lot of clapping.

I walked out toward the mound and the Chicago kids, who were standing between the mound and home plate. I asked the Chicago kids if I should go all of the way to the pitching rubber or if I should stand in front of the mound, the same distance that a Little League pitcher would throw. Of course, they said go to the mound. When I did, the crowd got a lot louder. I started wondering if I'd be able to throw a strike.

Then, I, Mo'ne, a city kid who plays sports with the boys, stood on the pitcher's mound at the MLB World Series. I set myself, went through my windup, and threw a perfect strike!

The crowd made this super-loud noise. That was kind of cool because I didn't know that many people from San Francisco would actually know me. I figured the people who knew me were just out on the East Coast.

Then I fist-pumped and smiled because all my years of hard work and sacrifice and practice had helped me throw a strike in front of all those people, even in the cold, and even when I hadn't practiced.

During the game, we sat in a box next to a lot of Giants fans. A couple of the Chicago kids were rooting for the Royals. Needless to say, the crowd drowned out their cheers.

The best part was there were a lot of Hall of Famers there—Willie Mays, Barry Bonds, Frank Robinson, and Hank Aaron. I got to meet Frank Robinson and Hank Aaron, but not Willie Mays or Barry Bonds. I asked them about Hunter Pence's swing. They told me it was kind of ugly, but that if it works for him, he should keep it. And then Hank Aaron and Frank Robinson both signed a baseball for me. We also got to meet Giancarlo Stanton from the Miami Marlins.

After the game, they gave me the World Series ball that I threw out, and they put an official sticker on it. I also got a Giants shirt, a signed bat from Clayton Kershaw, and Matt Kemp's jersey, and I gave him a signed *Sports Illustrated* and a baseball undershirt, so it was trade for trade. And I brought home some hotel lotion.

That weekend was up there with the Texas Little League game as the best time of my life.

I saw Laila Ali again toward the end of the month, when we presented an award together at the Soul Train Awards in Las Vegas. Someone had written a script for us to say, so we had to practice it together.

I was nervous. But Miss Laila told me that if I took deep breaths it would help keep me from being so nervous. I got to say who won the award for Song of the Year, which was Pharrell Williams, for "Happy." I wanted to meet him, but he wasn't there.

I did meet some other famous singers and celebrities, though. I met the singers Tank, Tiggers, and Joe; the rappers Lady of Rage and MC Lyte; and Judge Mathis from TV. I also met Boyz II Men, from South Philly.

I started learning that most celebrities are just like regular people.

....

Later in October, I was invited to participate in a ceremony honoring Malala Yousafzai. If you don't know Malala's story, I really think you should learn about her. She's the youngest person ever to be given the Nobel Peace Prize, one of the most important awards in the world. She won it when she was seventeen.

Malala grew up in Pakistan at a time when the Taliban—which is a religious organization that became powerful in politics there—made a law that only boys could be educated and that girls had to stop going to school. Malala kept going to school anyway—her father owned some schools.

When she was nine, she started blogging about the bad things the Taliban was doing in her community. As she became older, she was posting on Facebook, going on the radio and TV, and giving interviews to magazines, to fight for education for girls. The Taliban hated her so much that they tried to kill her by shooting her three times—one of the bullets even went into her forehead.

But Malala lived.

And as soon as she recovered, she continued fighting for girls.

Malala is so brave that she is an inspiration to me. I may be able to throw a mean fastball, but I don't know what I would do if I couldn't go to school, or if I had to make a choice between going to school and staying alive.

So I was super, super nervous when the National Constitution Center, in Philadelphia, invited me to read a passage from her book *I Am Malala: The Story of the Girl Who Stood Up for Education and Was Shot by the Taliban*. I had to get up in front of a lot of people and read passages she wrote about wearing a uniform to school, and the Taliban. I didn't want to mess anything up. Before I read the passage, I was so nervous my teeth were chattering.

I got to meet Malala and a lot of other teenagers who were doing meaningful things. It was a really good experience.

On Thanksgiving, all of the Dragons were invited to be in the Macy's Thanksgiving Day Parade—the biggest parade in the country. There are balloons and floats and marching bands and celebrities—all sorts of stuff. But I didn't know that my teammates and I, we would be in the front of the whole entire parade.

The night before, we went to the Hard Rock Café, and I had a burger. After that we went to the Big Apple Circus at Lincoln Center, but Scott and Jahli kept giving away the secrets to the tricks. On the way there, we took a picture in Times Square. We had to wake up at five to be ready for the parade. We took a bus to the start of the parade and lined up for an hour and a half while they staged the entire parade. While we were waiting, we got to run around with the crowd and throw confetti. After the parade began we talked to each other because people were waving more at the clowns than they were at us. It was cold, so afterward we went to Macy's to try to watch Becky G. perform her song "Shower" in the parade, but we had missed her. We drank hot chocolate and took pictures with Meghan Trainor, the Vamps, and Nick Jonas.

I never expected any of this. But I really didn't expect to be invited to the White House on the night that they lit the national Christmas tree in President's Park across the street. But after my school day ended on December 3, my mom and I headed to the train station to go to Washington, DC.

When we got there that night, we were directed into a big tent, which was like the greenroom, but they called it the "talent tent." Everybody was rehearsing their acts. I practiced my part with a very nice assistant who stood in for Mrs. Obama—she called Mrs. Obama "FLOTUS," which is short for First Lady of the United States. I also got to meet Tom Hanks, and I took a picture with him. On the way to the hotel after rehearsal, my mom told our driver that I am a big fan of Fifth Harmony, and the driver told my mom she'd tell them when she picked them up to take them to the tent for rehearsal the next morning. It was a little awkward. I don't know if she did.

Early that next morning, we went back to the tent for a second rehearsal and to practice the grand finale. I was pretty nervous. The singers Patti LaBelle, who's from South Philly, Ne-Yo, and Nico and Vinz were there. I got to meet Ne-Yo, and he was really nice.

At one point we were all standing around and I was minding my business, kind of nervous, singing to myself.

"What song are you singing?" my mom asked.

"'Am I Wrong?'" I said. Then I realized it was Nico and Vinz's song. I think it got in my head because Jahli played it in Williamsport so much.

"That's amazing!" Nico and Vinz said.

So I started talking to Nico and Vinz. Since they're from Norway, they don't really understand baseball, so they were asking me a lot of questions about how the game is played.

Then I got on my phone and started playing a baseball game. I didn't realize it, but while I was playing, Fifth Harmony walked in. While my mom was getting a cup of coffee, she went and told them that I wanted to meet them but was scared.

"Is that the pitcher?" they asked.

"Yes, that's her right there," my mom said.

They came over to introduce themselves right when I had put a big piece of Dubble Bubble in my mouth! I shoved the wad of gum into the side of my cheek so I wouldn't embarrass myself trying to chew it. They were super, super nice to me, and we took a few pictures before they went to rehearse.

"You, my friend, are an inspiration," one of them said. That was pretty awesome.

Everyone had been very friendly. There were a lot of "Good lucks" and fist bumps all throughout the day.

When we came back for the live show later that evening, we had to wait for a long time in traffic because the president was coming and the police had blocked off all the cars.

Finally, we got to the talent tent. The president and Mrs. Obama were in a different tent, and Sasha and Malia were in a whole nother tent that was connected to their parents' tent but not ours.

We got to go into the tent where the president and First Lady were sitting. President Obama said, "Mo'ne Davis!"

When he called out my name, I saw Sasha and Malia peeking into the room from their tent. We took a picture with the president and the First Lady.

President Obama said, "You should come back one day and I'll challenge you to a game of H-O-R-S-E."

"He's a little competitive," Mrs. Obama said. "I'm rooting for you to win."

I laughed.

It was pretty chilly that night, but a lot of parents and children still came to the show. While they were getting seated, we all sat in the talent tent. Right before Tom Hanks went onstage, I remembered that he had been in the women's baseball film *A League of Their Own*.

"Filming that was fun," he said. "All we did was hit baseballs and catch fly balls."

If you've never seen *A League of Their Own*, it's a film about an all-girl baseball league. Tom Hanks plays a baseball coach, and he makes one of the players on his team of all women cry after she made a mistake.

"Are you crying?" he says to her. "There's no crying in baseball."

That's become a famous line.

Tom Hanks was the MC of the show with his wife, Rita Wilson.

The ceremony started when they showed this big video of everyone who was going to appear. I was sitting next to one of the dads of the Fifth Harmony girls.

"Hey, I wasn't in the video!" I told him. Just when I said that, the video announcer said, "And special guest Mo'ne Davis!" and I heard the crowd cheer.

When the president and the First Family came out, we counted down, and red and green lights came on. One of the cool things about the tree-lighting ceremony is that they got all these girls to code the design of the main tree and fifty-six other trees all around the White House grounds.

After the tree was lit, a bunch of the different artists performed. Fifth Harmony sang the song "All I Want for Christmas Is You."

While I was waiting to go onstage, Mrs. Obama told me to come sit on the couch next to her so we could talk.

"We were watching you in the office," she said. "You were amazing." Then she asked me about school and whether basketball had started yet.

A little while later, Tom Hanks introduced me to read 'Twas the Night Before Christmas with Mrs. Obama. Fortunately, by now I was used to big crowds. And since I had read for Malala, I wasn't that nervous.

Mrs. Obama gave me a high five when we finished, and I went back into the talent tent. Then Ne-Yo performed.

Right before we were going to go back onstage to be in the finale, I was talking to another Fifth Harmony dad.

"You throw seventy miles per hour?" he said.

"Yeah . . ."

"That's so cool to be throwing against guys that fast!" he said. "That's amazing!"

I never realized how many people knew about me!

During the finale everyone was on the stage singing

and dancing to "Jingle Bells." The First Family came up on the other end and walked down the line, hugging everyone and shaking their hands. Sasha and Malia came up with them.

"Oh my gosh, that's amazing what you did," they said. "You're an inspiration. We were watching you. Keep doing what you're doing."

Their whole family is super tall. I didn't know that President Obama or Mrs. Obama was that tall. Sasha and Malia are tall, too.

After we came down from the stage, one of the Fifth Harmony girls was like, "Where were you? We were looking for you. We were going to dance with you on the stage."

I was standing way down at the other end, dancing next to Santa Claus.

After the show was over, we couldn't leave the tent because people were protesting nearby, plus the First Family had to leave, so the streets were blocked off for a while. It was late and I was ready to go home.

But while we were waiting to go to the train, good things happened. One of the Fifth Harmony moms got her daughter to follow me on Instagram and Twitter. Then I got to dance with one of them to their song "Sledgehammer," and one of them made a video of us. I got to dance with Ne-Yo, too.

When I went back to school the next day, I told my friends about everything that had happened. When I told them that the president wanted to play H-O-R-S-E, they laughed.

"He's the president," they said. "You have to let him win."

"But Mrs. Obama said don't," I said, "so I don't know what I'm supposed to do."

I have gotten to do a lot of things and meet a lot of famous people since I played with the Taney Dragons in the Little League World Series. I hadn't expected any of it, but I wouldn't trade a single moment.

CHAPTER 16

A GOOD PATH

IF SOMEONE WOULD HAVE TOLD ME THAT THIS WOULD BE MY life, I never would have believed them. I still don't always really understand what is happening and why so many people are inspired by me.

I'm super, super excited that so many good things are happening to show me how all the risks I've taken, sacrifices I've made, and hard work can pay off. Because it hasn't always been easy getting up at two and three in the morning to do homework, or to scramble all around town to get someplace in time for a game. It's not always fun to have to take the bus for almost two hours to school and almost two hours home. I don't always like to miss birthday parties, water parks, and other family events in the summer and on the weekends because I have to go to practice or play in tournaments.

It's hard to believe it's paying off like this, but I know that experiences like this will not go on forever.

I'm learning a lot. For one thing, I'm learning what a big difference it makes to have people like Coach Steve in your life, who see your talent and take an interest in you. I hope that my teammates and I have shown the adults that inner-city kids want to play baseball and can be as good at it as kids who have a lot more money than we do. We deserve to have opportunities to play sports and get a great education.

It's also important to have role models and people who inspire you, especially when you're a girl. From my mom to Miss Mamie Johnson to my favorite WNBA stars, Maya Moore and Skyler Diggins, to Mrs. Obama, I've met a lot of girls and women who have inspired me and who I've always dreamed about meeting. They have all been very nice to me and have encouraged me to keep going.

I had always hoped to be on TV, but I didn't expect to become a role model at such a young age. I hope that I can keep encouraging other girls.

It's sad to me, but a lot of girls haven't played sports. If you haven't played sports, I think you should just try to see how you like it, and if you like it, keep doing it. Try different sports, so you can find out what you like and what you're good at. But don't just try it for a day and say, "I don't like this." Try it out for a few months. Even if it's hard or you're not good at first, just focus on the fun you are having with each one of your teammates. And if you find out you don't like sports, just try to be active, so you can stay in shape.

For girls who play sports, I think that girls should be able to play sports with the boys, especially when there's not a girls' team. A girl can be as good as the boys, or even better. I think that boys should be nice to girls who play against them, and play fair—they might learn something. Girls can even make boys want to learn to "throw like a girl."

In sports and at my school, I've learned a lot about leadership, and how important it is to set a good example and do the right things so that other people can follow what you did. When you're a role model, you know you're on a good path to doing something special, and whatever that is, you'll encourage more people to do it. When people keep telling you you're doing something good, just keep doing it.

On top of being a role model for girls, I want to be a role model to tell people not to quit things too soon. I think you should hang in there a little longer, because you may find you like it after all. Look at all the things I would have missed out on if I had quit baseball way back when I was ten.

Life isn't always easy, and sometimes you're gonna fail. You have to fail in order to make it somewhere. Everything can't be all success. If you only had success and you lost the first game ever in your life, you wouldn't know how to handle it because you had never lost before.

But failure is actually a good way to succeed. There's always gonna be the setback in sports and in life that will help you do better the next time. Like if there is a championship game and you lose, then next year you're gonna work twice as hard as you did before because you want to win that championship.

When I grow up, if I play in the MLB, I would probably like to play for the Dodgers because they always seem to have a good team, and they're in LA. LA is really fun. For one thing, there's no snow.

On top of being a pitcher, I think it would be fun to play shortstop.

But my real dream is to go to the University of Connecticut and be the point guard on the basketball team, and then go into the WNBA.

All of this is a long ways away. But one thing I know for sure—hard work can take you anywhere.

ACKNOWLEDGMENTS

Even though I have gotten a lot of attention, I couldn't have been successful without my teams at home, at school, in my community, and in the Monarch and Taney dugouts.

To my mom and my stepdad: You have loved me, helped me, fed me, sacrificed, paid my entry fees, bought my shorts and T-shirts and uniforms, washed my dirty clothes, driven me all over the city and up and down the East Coast, stayed in boring hotel rooms, laughed at my cheesy jokes, stayed on top of my homework, sometimes yelled at me, and even indulged my sneaker obsession. I'm grateful.

My brothers and sister have shared my ups and downs, watched crazy Vines with me, put up with me studying for hours in the bathroom so I can get some peace and quiet, tolerated the fact that sometimes money was tight because it was used to buy me new cleats, and dealt with the times that Mom or Squirt wasn't there because they were traveling with me. Thank you so much, I love you. Thank you, especially, to Mahogany for dealing with my messy bedroom.

I'm grateful to my grandmothers, aunts, uncles, cousins, and other family members and friends, who have come to my games and encouraged me—especially to my cousin Mark for taking me to Anderson and giving me the chance to meet Coach Steve in the first place.

It's super, super important to have grown-ups in your life who can see the potential in you and help you reach your dreams. Everyone needs a Coach Steve who can love you, teach you, protect you, help you, and encourage you to try new things and to be your best. It really means a lot that you've been in my corner—I couldn't have gotten here without you. Thank you for introducing me to Jackie Robinson, believing in inner-city kids, and showing the world what we're capable of. Miss Robin, thank you for opening your heart and your home to me, Mo'ne, your second daughter. Stephanie, thank you so much for letting me sleep in your bedroom.

Thank you to Mr. Shawn, who runs Marian Anderson, for creating such a wonderful environment for kids to grow, develop, and explore our talents. I wish every young person had a place like Anderson to hang out and play sports at.

I want to express my appreciation to my other Anderson Monarchs coaches, Coach Charles, Coach Elliott, Coach Ike, and Coach John, who are important leaders of our team, but who I didn't write about because it would have made my story too complicated.

Coach Alex, thank you for coaching the Taney Dragons and for believing in me in tough games, such as against the West. That meant a lot to me. It's unbelievable to think that we made it to the top!

My teammates and I, we are like each other's family. We help each other become better players, encourage each other, and keep each other calm when things are hard and we're frustrated. Oh, and I can't forget how much we joke, and laugh, and act silly, and prank each other, and just have fun! I especially want to thank my teammates on the Anderson Monarchs, who have been part of my extended family since I was seven.

Everyone knows that Scott has an incredible memory. Thank you for helping me remember some of the details I've forgotten. You have been my partner in crime in every big thing that has happened to me on the field.

It's been so much fun sharing those experiences with you. You sick about it or nah? Jahli and Zion, you always come through in the clutch, even for this book. Thank you so much.

I'm really grateful to Jack and Jared for having the dream of going to the World Series and for being determined to make your dream come true. I'm so glad I got to come along for the ride!

Every now and then angels show up in your life. Mr. Tony and Miss Jean Vernon, I thank you for providing financial support to allow me to get a great education.

Every kid deserves to go to a great school and have teachers who love them and make their day fun. Dr. Sands, thank you for seeing the potential in me when I first came to visit Springside, for coming to Williamsport, for throwing the watch parties during the World Series, and for protecting me now that so many people remember my name.

Thank you also to all of my teachers and school leaders—but especially, to Miss Posner, Miss Sakovics, Mr. Dreisbach, and Mr. Budde—for believing in the power of girls. Thank you, Miss McCrae, for helping to make me feel so comfortable when I first came to Springside.

Coach Brady, thank you for helping me to become a better basketball player. (Sorry to disappoint you about the lacrosse.) It was also so nice to see your face when I was retiring my jersey.

Miss Davis—I mean, Miss Jackson—thank you for protecting me.

Qayyah and Yirah, I love you even though you wake me up too early to go to the courts and play basketball. You have helped me sharpen my game and you've been my female friends at the court. Hope to see you in the WNBA!

Abby, Alexia, Destiny, and Nahla, thank you for being such wonderful friends and dealing with my big obsession with Fifth Harmony.

Thank you to all the members of my Springside Chestnut Hill Academy community who drove up to Williamsport, or came to a watch party, or the parade, or another event to cheer us on.

I am so grateful to all the people from Philly who drove all the way to Williamsport, came to watch parties, cheered us on, and created Taney-mania back home. I especially want to thank Mayor Nutter for being so supportive of me and my Taney teammates—from the watch party at City Hall to our welcome home celebration at LOVE Park to the victory parade.

It's kind of unbelievable to know that so many people around the country rooted for us. Thank you to all of you, especially all the girls who I inspired and who now inspire me.

Thank you to all the MLB and WNBA teams and players who have motivated and spent time with me and my teammates, especially the Philadelphia Phillies.

What is left to say about Jackie Robinson? Thank you for inspiring me to be my best, showing me how to ignore the bad things in life and listen to the good, for setting an example for how to be classy, and for teaching us how to steal home.

It always means a lot to know that someone who looks like you do and comes from where you come from can make it to the top. Marian Anderson, thank you for showing me what girls from South Philly can do, and for being a role model to show me how far you can go when people see your potential and open the door for you.

Thank you to Miss Mamie Johnson, for dreaming that I could one day be the first lady in the MLB. I never thought I would ever meet anyone like me, but then I met you. I am grateful for all your encouragement.

Thank you to the team at HarperCollins for believing that a girl like me would have something to say. Miss Pam, thank you for the pictures that you took of me in Washington—one of them is my background on my computer screen—and for helping me put my best foot forward. Miss Hilary, thank you for helping me organize my thoughts and find my voice in this book.

I don't know very much about business yet, but thank you to my book agent, Larry Weissman; my manager, Dolores Robinson; my financial advisor, Edward Platcher; and my lawyers, Mark Aronchik and Jack Kinney, for managing it.

President and Mrs. Obama, I can't believe I got to meet you and read with you. Thank you so much for the invitation and for spending time and encouraging me. It was a dream come true—actually, it was a dream I hadn't even had yet. Mr. President, I'm ready for that game of H-O-R-S-E.

Hilary Beard would like to thank:

Mo'ne, I know that talking to your friends, practicing your curveball, and raining threes are all a lot more fun than writing a book, especially under a deadline as tight as ours. Thank you for opening your heart and world to me. You're amazing! And don't forget, if you can squeeze it in, you'd be great at my favorite sport, tennis.

Lakeisha and Squirt, thank you for trusting me with your daughter and her story. You have so much to be proud of. Working with you has been a joy.

Coach Steve, what a different place the world would be if every child had an adult in their village with a vision as grand as yours and a heart to match. Thanks to you and Robin for helping me as well.

My appreciation to Priscilla Sands, Meadow Sakovics, Saburah Posner, Miss Jackson, Josh Budde, Mr. Driesbach, Coach Brady, and the rest of the Springside Chestnut Hill Academy community—you made everything so easy.

April Eugene, thank you for turning around so many transcripts so quickly and over Thanksgiving and weekends.

Madeleine Morel, I'm grateful that you continue to think of me.

Ralph Montilla and Alex Beard, and Kailey and Jadon Beard, you are my inspiration.

ABOUT THE AUTHORS

Mo'ne Davis started participating in organized sports at the age of seven. She plays baseball, soccer, and basketball and is an honor-roll student at her school in Philadelphia. She is in eighth grade.

Hilary Beard is an award-winning writer, author, editor, and book collaborator. She lives in Philadelphia.